Well, that's something I never thought I'd see. With my mouth hanging open, I watched two completely hot men tumble around on the sidewalk in front of my first-floor apartment, trying to beat the crap out of each other.

Yes, I did understand that the proper reaction would be to panic or feel angered by their immature behavior, but I wasn't just anyone. Remember, I was once the girl no one looked at except with pity or disgust. Yes, I compensated with my personality and still had lots of girlfriends, but getting male attention felt alien, and this was no exception. Italy's hottest actor and America's sexiest bachelor were fighting over me.

This is definitely strange. And so amazingly hot. Wait. Am I evil for thinking that?

praise for mimi jean's
romantic comedies

"an intense, utterly riveting book that I literally could not put down, that kept my heart racing."

—*Chapter 5* on *Fugly*

"Smart, heart-wrenching and wonderfully sexy, this is contemporary romance at its finest. Pamfiloff pulls expertly at the heartstrings with a sassy heroine and the most compelling hero I've read in years."

—*USA Today* bestselling author Lauren Layne on *Tailored for Trouble*

"I would give this book a galaxy of stars if I could. It was beautiful. It was thought provoking. It was sad, funny, sexy, but most of all it was riveting. I could not put it down. Absolutely fantastic."

—*A Goddess & Her Books* on *Fugly*

"Swoony, sexy, and laugh-out-loud funny! Bennett Wade is an absolutely delicious hero—and this book left me wanting more."

—*New York Times* bestselling author Laura Kaye on *Tailored for Trouble*

"Pamfiloff's skilled pacing ramps up the tension and attraction between Bennett and Taylor as they crisscross the globe together, and their consummation feels like a well-deserved payoff for them and the reader."

—*Publishers Weekly* on *Tailored for Trouble*

"Mimi Jean Pamfiloff has a way with words that keeps you laughing and enjoying the story as it grips you and draws you in."

—*Fresh Fiction* on *Tailored for Trouble*

other works by

mimi jean pamfiloff

COMING SOON:
GOD OF WINE
(Immortal Matchmakers Series, Book 3)
THE TEN CLUB
(The King Series, Book 5)

AVAILABLE NOW:
FUGLY (Standalone/Contemporary Romance)

IMMORTAL MATCHMAKERS, INC. SERIES
(Standalones/Paranormal/Humor)
The Immortal Matchmakers (Book1)
Tommaso (Book 2)

THE FATE BOOK SERIES
(Standalones/New Adult Suspense/Humor)
Fate Book
Fate Book Two

THE HAPPY PANTS SERIES
(Standalones/Romantic Comedy)
The Happy Pants Café (Prequel)
Tailored for Trouble (Book 2)

TO: Kimberly

it's a fugly life

Mimi Jean Pamfiloff

a Mimi Boutique Novel

wishing you infinite smiles whenever you need them.

M.J.M

Cover Design by Earthly Charms (www.earthlycharms.com)
Development Editing by Latoya C. Smith (lcsliterary.com)
Line Editing and Proof Reading by Pauline Nolet
(www.paulinenolet.com)
Formatting by BB eBooks (bbebooksthailand.com)

Like "Free" Pirated Books?

Then Ask Yourself This Question: WHO ARE THESE PEOPLE I'M HELPING?

What sort of person or organization would put up a website that uses stolen work (or encourages its users to share stolen work) in order to make money for themselves, either through website traffic or direct sales? **Haven't you ever wondered?**

Putting up thousands of pirated books onto a website or creating those anonymous ebook file sharing sites takes time and resources. Quite a lot, actually.

So who are these people? Do you think they're decent, ethical people with good intentions? Why do they set up camp anonymously in countries where they can't easily be touched? And the money they make from advertising every time you go to their website, or through selling stolen work, **what are they using it for? The answer is you don't know.** They could be terrorists, organized criminals, or just greedy bastards. But one thing we DO know is that **THEY ARE CRIMINALS** who don't care about you, your family, or me and mine. **And their intentions can't be good.**

And every time you illegally share or download a book, YOU ARE HELPING these people. Meanwhile, people like me, who work to support a family and children, are left wondering why anyone would condone this.

So please, please ask yourself who YOU are HELPING when you support ebook piracy and then ask yourself who you are HURTING.

And for those who legally pur-chased/borrowed/obtained my work from a reputable retailer (not sure, just ask me!) muchas thank yous! You rock.

dedication

This book is dedicated to the readers who wrote and shared their own stories after reading *FUGLY*. You gave me a lot to think about in my own journey, and for this, I felt I owed you the rest of Lily's story.

it's a fugly life

chapter one

No, no, no. What did he just fucking say? I stared at the ass-faced reporter blocking my way to the church. A sadistic smirk stretched across his lips while his crew filmed my reaction. They hoped I'd cry for the entire world on my wedding day, didn't they?

Maybe I would.

"Tell us, Miss Snow, how does it feel?" He urged the cameraman closer and shoved the microphone an inch from my face. "How does it feel knowing your fiancé cheated on you last night?"

The bastard cheated on me? The night before our wedding? I tried to blink away my tears, but his words felt like a red-hot poker through my collapsing heart. After everything that had happened, every tear shed, every moment of struggle, and the promises made, I couldn't believe it had all led to this: emotional annihilation.

What did you expect, Lily? Princes don't fall for frogs. Not in real life. He wanted a beautiful life, a perfect life. He wanted a beautiful wife and beautiful babies. I couldn't give him those things.

I dropped my bouquet, smoothed down the front of my white dress, and lifted my chin. "It feels like shit." I turned away from the church, ignoring the roar of the press and the clicking of cameras, leaving behind my last shred of belief in happy-ever-afters.

Those don't exist. They never did.

Six Weeks Earlier

Today was huge. Huger than huge. Okay, it wasn't really, but I needed to remind myself that the little milestones in life were as important as the champagne-worthy events. For example, just three months ago, I'd opened my very own boutique in downtown Santa Barbara. Think eclectic, handmade clothing and accessories, sort of like that one aisle at Whole Foods with the mishmash of tie-dyed scarves and hemp bracelets. Not my lifelong dream, but my products were made by women, for women, and I loved the idea of making money while helping people. After three months, I'd gotten the helping part down, but not the making-money part. Sales were the pits, and I'd already received notice of a rent increase at the end of the year.

You'll figure it out, Lily. You always do. I drew a happy face on the puppies and kittens calendar stuck to the wall behind the register. It was important to stay positive and focused.

My smile faded as it dawned on me that today also marked another event. *Six months.* Six months since I'd seen Maxwell Cole—cocky, SOB billionaire and quite possibly the most hypnotically sexy and complex man in the world—and asked him to forgive me for some pretty awful things I had done.

He hadn't.

And it had been the roughest time of my life. Rougher than working for the man. Rougher than falling in love with him—my boss—a man so far out of my league that I hadn't been able to believe he wanted me back. And certainly rougher than the day I effectively tanked his multibillion-dollar company. An edgy, cosmetics juggernaut he'd built with his own two hands.

And I fucked it up.

Yep.

With my own two lips, aka my big fat mouth. All because I believed—erroneously—that he didn't have feelings for me.

Crap, Lily. I blew out a breath and ran a hand over the top of my hair, smoothing back the loose strands of my ponytail. "Stop it. Just stop it." I'd already decided months ago to be done with the self-flagellation. I couldn't go back. I couldn't undo the past. And either way, I'd moved on.

"Every journey starts with one step," I muttered to myself and put another smiley face on my calendar. And as of today, I'd made it six months. I'd put my life back together and was even dati—

The cluster of silver bells above the front door to my tiny shop jingled to welcome the first customer of the day.

"Welcome to Lily's Pad. Let me know if I can help y..." I glanced up from behind the register and lost my grip on the pen in my hand. "Max?"

"Hello, Lily." His deep, exquisitely masculine voice washed over me like a tsunami of emotional shock.

"Max, what are you doing here?" My eyes stuck on his face, drinking in every virile detail. Maxwell Cole wasn't what people would call a handsome man. Handsome implied someone who might be nice looking or pleasing to look at. This infamous, thirty-four-year-old billionaire was so much more. Women saw him and couldn't look away from his six-three frame, underwear model physique, hazel eyes and chiseled jawline that gave him a godlike appearance. It was the same stunning good looks he'd used to build his multibillion-dollar cosmetics company. He used to model in his ads. Semi-nude. Yes, total eye candy for women of every age.

"I heard you're hiring a part-time assistant." He pointed to the sign in the window with one of those muscular arms I used to enjoy wrapped around my midriff when he took me from behind with his substantial co—

Don't torture yourself. He dumped you hard. Obviously, the man was here for a reason, although I couldn't fathom what that reason might be.

He continued, "I also heard you might be looking for a husband. But I don't have any experience. Think you might consider me anyway?" He shoved a hand in his jeans pocket and looked at me with a wickedly sexy grin.

Huh? My mind couldn't quite absorb his words or their meaning. I was far too busy realizing how much I'd missed him and how fucking delicious he looked. He wore these expensive sexy jeans that hung just right on his hips and a dark gray button-down shirt that said, "Yeah, I've got money. Yeah, my body is a temple of male perfection. No, you can't have me—I'm for looking only, ladies." In other words, everything about the man screamed unattainable. His dark messy hair, his overgrown stubble—not quite a beard—his full kissable lips and jaw and chin and everything about him was...perfect.

I swear, that man could wear a neon yellow jockstrap and orange traffic cone on his head and still look like he'd strolled off a runway.

Wait. He just asked me to marry him?

Nope. Nope. I'm dreaming. I have fallen and hit my head, and any moment I'm going to wake up with a splitting headache.

I suddenly realized that Max's mouth kept moving, but I hadn't heard a word.

"Sorry? Could you repeat that?" I blinked some more.

He stepped forward, putting himself on the other side of the counter, opposite me. "I know I should've called. I wanted to a million times. But I needed time to sort out a few things." His smile faded, and the look in his hazel eyes hardened.

Did he mean he needed time to forgive me? I didn't know, but clearly he had, and I felt a huge weight lift from my soul. I hadn't even realized I'd been carrying it around.

I nodded my head. "I understand. I did ruin your company."

"Fuck the company. I was going to let it all go anyway. You and I both know my mother needed to be gone from my life." His mother, the cruelest piece of sadistic human-shit on the planet, had owned fifty-one percent of his company, making it difficult for him to keep a distance. Still, I had to believe that if not for me, things would've gone down differently. Maybe he could've found an investor to buy her out or something. But because of me, he'd been forced to sell Cole Cosmetics to a Canadian competitor for half its original value. I hated thinking about all that. It made my stomach knot with guilt.

"You're only saying that to make me feel less crappy," I said softly. "That company was everything to you."

"No. You were everything to me and you still are. I realized it when I watched them pry your bloody body from your car with a crowbar. Do you have any idea what that did to me?"

Oh. That. It wasn't that I'd forgotten, but I rarely thought of that day anymore. Mostly because losing Max overshadowed all of the surrounding drama. But seven months ago, right as everything blew up with his company, a news van chased me on the highway near Chicago, hoping to get a story about my relationship with my infamous boss. I plowed my convertible Mini into the center divider and made mincemeat out of my face.

Now, before you start thinking that it must've left me with a horrible disfigurement,

I'll have you know two things. One, I was born with an extremely ugly face. I mean nose from hell, an unusually large chin, and—well, let's just say that small children often cried when they looked at me. "Mommy! It's a monster." Think Chaka from *Land of the Lost* but with a very petite body, nice teeth, and long wavy blonde hair. That was me.

Now are you seeing why I couldn't quite believe my international sex symbol of a boss loved me?

Moving on to point number two: The accident did leave me scarred—forehead, chin, and one side of my nose—the place where the side mirror of my car broke off and impacted. But by then I had already made up my mind to fix my ugly face against Max's wishes. Long story short, when the accident happened, Max—despite being furious with me for what I did to his company—still made sure I was put back together by the best. Now people stared but they didn't retch, and with a little makeup, I could cover most of the scars.

"I'm so sorry, Max. I can't say it enough times." Yes, I had apologized to him already— after my accident, after he'd made sure I was put back together, after he had to sell his company, and after I'd made a mess of our relationship. But my plea for forgiveness fell on cold ears. He could hardly look me in the eyes that day.

"I'm the one who is sorry." Max planted his arms on the counter and leaned in, his eyes filled with a sternness that meant he wasn't messing around. "None of those events would've happened if I'd simply told you how much I love you and asked you to marry me. I should've been stronger, but I wasn't."

He was taking the blame? Him? "But...but...I...you...you were so angry and..." I shook my head. I was the one who messed it all up.

He grabbed my hand from across the counter and squeezed it. "I was hurt because you didn't trust me, Lily. You didn't believe in us—fuck." He drew a breath. "I didn't come here to rehash this crap."

"Remind me again; why are you here?"

"Marry me, Lily. Because I love you. And I never want to let you go."

Every part of my body and soul swelled with emotion and disbelief. "You *really* want to marry me?" I said, trying to get it all straight in my head.

He slid a small black box from his pocket and opened it to reveal a gorgeous diamond ring.

I was too excited and overwhelmed to actually look at it or make my lips move or get my feet to walk around the counter. I wanted to kiss him and cry and tell him how damned sorry I was for fucking up our relationship.

"Well?" Those hazel eyes drilled into me.

I held up my index finger. "I think I'm going to be sick." I turned and ran for the back of my little store. I flipped on the bathroom lights and leaned my body over the toilet, feeling the wave of nerves hit me hard.

"Lily?"

I panted, but nothing came out. *Breathe, breathe, breathe.* The wave passed, and I stood upright. Slowly, I turned my gaze toward the tall, muscularly framed, beautiful man standing in the doorway, with one eyebrow cocked and his thick arms crossed over his broad chest.

"This is not going how I imagined." He flashed a cocky little smile.

Oh shit. Reply. Reply, stupid! "Yes! Yes. Wait. No!"

"No?" His head jerked back.

Fuck! "I can't accept your proposal."

He blinked at me. "This is definitely not how I expected it to go."

I stepped back an inch, needing to put distance between us in any way possible. He had no idea what I'd been through these last six months. He had no idea how hard it had been to get up every day and not cry or hate myself for what I'd done to him, to us. But I'd finally pulled my life together a few crumbs at a time.

I'd...moved on. At least, I was trying.

I tugged down on the hem of my pink sweater and lifted my chin. "I'm sorry," I said with a firm tone, "but I can't marry you."

He stared with a scowl I knew so, so well, reminding me of when he was Mr. Cole, my boss. My hot dickhead of a boss with a very strange secret.

I inhaled deeply. What I had to say next would not please him. Not in the least. But he and I had always been honest with each other. It was the foundation of our relationship and what I loved most about us. Okay, that and the sex.

I swallowed and looked down at my pink flats—yes, they went with my sweater and my pink jeans. Why hadn't I worn something more serious today? Because saying what I had to say next, dressed like a piece of Pepto, made me feel ridiculous. I needed a black leather jacket or a flame-retardant suit for this.

"I, uh..." I cleared my throat. "I'm engaged already. Well...mostly." I hadn't officially said yes to my boyfriend, but I'd intended to.

"What! Who? Who, Lily!" Max yelled.

I cringed, knowing full well he would not understand. With one eye closed and the other squinting, I turned my head to the side, preparing for a giant explosion. Boom! Male ego everywhere.

"Patricio Ferrari?" I eked out.

Max's face seemed to inflate like a giant angry red balloon. "The *fucking* actor?" he roared.

It wasn't a question. Not really. Maxwell Cole knew exactly who Patricio Ferrari was. Nope. They weren't friends.

"Yes," I whispered with my eyes closed, "the actor. Who else?"

Max opened his mouth to speak, pointed his finger in my face, and then snapped his mouth shut and looked away. I watched while he repeated the action—open mouth, point, close mouth, look away, open mouth, point, close mouth...

"Max." I stepped forward and gently grabbed his arm. "Please try to understand. You didn't want me. You said goodbye." Or at least that was how it seemed at the time when I'd said something like, "I am so sorry. Please give me another chance." And he'd said something like, "Thanks for coming by, but I have to meet with my lawyers."

"But you..." he snarled. "You...Patricio. Really?" He shook his head in disgust.

"Max, I'm sorry, but yes, really. He loves me, and he makes me happy." Patricio and I cooked dinners together and watched silly movies. We wore stupid hats and rollerbladed at Venice beach. We took off to the mountains and went skiing. I couldn't remember having so much fun and that was because I never knew how. Not before Patricio. He'd introduced me to a part of myself I needed. And he taught me how to breathe again. His looks weren't so bad either.

Max ran his hands through his messy dark hair. "Do you fucking love him, Lily?"

I didn't even need to think about the answer. *Yes! Maybe? No, definitely yes*. But did I love him like I loved Max, with pure chaotic passion? No. Patricio and I were more like friends, and after having my heart decimated by Max, that made me feel safe. Yes, Patricio was definitely the type of guy I should marry and could grow to love more over time.

"Yes. I love him," I replied without specifying the type of love. It wasn't any of Max's business.

Max's rapid pulse ticked away on his neck. "How...but...me...but..."

To see such an articulate, opinionated, stubborn-as-hell man like Max fail to find his words tore out my heart.

"Six months," he growled like a horrible accusation. "Six fucking months!"

"Stop yelling at me," I snapped. "Not when I could say the same to you, Max. Six months. Where were you?" I hadn't heard a word since that day I asked him to forgive me, about a month after the accident.

"I was taking care of some very important things."

"Can you be any vaguer?" I asked.

"What does it matter what I was doing? Because clearly you were keeping yourself occupied."

Jerkface. Why did he expect me to sit around for half a year like a helpless, lovesick woman? That was not me. I was the type of person who picked herself up after she fell down.

As for Patricio, he was a very intense man who pursued his desires with passion. No different than Max. Ironically, Patricio and I had met at a party in Milan right before Max and I started our relationship. Anyway, Patricio and I had danced at that party and had fun. He didn't care about my presurgery looks or my fameless status. And a month after my Maxwell-meltdown slash very public breakup, Patricio somehow tracked down my number and asked me out for a drink. I said no at first. And the second and third and fourth times, too. Finally, a few months ago, I felt ready to take a step forward and move on. I accepted. Patricio made it clear on the very first date that he knew Max had broken my heart. "I don't care if you still love that asshole. I am here, claiming my stake. I want you, Lily. And I know what you've been through. I know what you must feel. But I also know what I feel. You," he'd kissed the top of my hand, "light up my life like no odder." He'd meant "other" but his Italian accent became exaggerated when he was excited or emotional. "Jess" instead of "yes." "Chew" instead of "you." "Hot" instead of "heart." *Jess, Leely. My hot belongs to chew.*

I loved it. He had a wild, crazy side, and when he had his breaks from filming, usually in L.A. where he now lived, I enjoyed spending time with him. No, Patricio and I didn't know each other extremely well, which was why his proposal seemed sudden, but like I said, we were good friends, we had fun, and what woman wouldn't want a famous, hot, Italian actor as a husband? We were a good match. Max, in comparison, made me feel lost to emotion, vulnerable, and...well, extremely aroused. *Stop that.*

I lifted my chin. "I'm sorry, Max. But you're six months too late. I'm marrying him."

"So you said yes." I could practically see the steam rising off the top of Max's head of messy brown hair. Perfectly messy, of course, because Max demanded perfection in everything he did.

"No." I had needed time to think. "But I will. Tonight."

A long moment passed while Max stared into my eyes. "Then you have to wait."

"Why would I do that?" Patricio loved me. I loved Patricio. No, as I explained, it wasn't the same type of love I once had with Max, but for as long as I breathed, I would never love anyone like that. But that was because the evolution of our relationship had been unlike anything else. Like many women, I first thought of Max as the indescribably sexy and driven man who appeared in all of those steamy ads for his company. Naked. Hand covering the goods. Ripped from head to toe. Words could not describe how much I worshipped him. Then we'd met when I interviewed for a sales position at his company, and I caught a glimpse of his ugly side. I hated the man. I hated how he looked at me, I hated looking at him, and I hated how he made me feel like the ugliest creature on the planet. Then he made me an offer I couldn't refuse and talked me into working for him. After that, we started to really see each other and ourselves for who we were.

I fell hard for him.

But Max and I had ended in self-destruction. Me with my ugly problems and him with his. Oh yes, that man had issues. Big, scary issues with fangs and wiry hair and an ice pick. We were so tainted by our fucking hang-ups that we were bound to end in a blazing fire of hurt. That had been the one sane thought I'd clung to these past six months: we were bad for each other, and it never would've worked. It didn't matter how much I loved him or he loved me.

"You owe me, Lily." Max's nostrils flared a bit.

I frowned. "I owe you what?"

"You took everything from me—my company, my sanity, and my peace of mind."

Whoa. "According to you—two seconds ago—you didn't want your company anymore, and before I came along, you were a slave to your...secret," I whispered that last word. I don't know why exactly, since it wasn't a secret anymore. Max's perfection-obsessed mother had psychologically abused him and his older sister, causing him to believe that anything unaesthetically pleasing was a cancer. His secret disorder was called cacophobia. He would experience extreme anxiety at the sight of ugliness. It sounded kind of funny until you were at the receiving end of that disgust or understood how hard it had made his life. His own sister had disowned them all, likely to save herself. Last I'd heard, Max was trying to find her.

As for his disorder? I had been Max's antidote. His desensitization therapy. Which was why he'd hired me. Okay—it was part of the reason. He believed in me and wanted to help me find my confidence. And while my outsides made him break out in a cold sweat, he found my insides irresistible. He eventually overcame his aversion, and we shared a few days of magic. Bliss. Heaven. Yes, for a few short moments we both believed we'd had a future together, without our uglies.

We'd been wrong.

"Lily." He gripped my shoulders. "We both know where this will go. Why make us suffer any more than we already have?"

"I don't know what you mean."

"I love you. More than anything, and I know you feel the same. So why put yourself or Patricio through any unnecessary turmoil?"

I felt enraged by his presumptive nature. He didn't own me. He knew nothing about what I'd been through. There was no way in *hell* I'd risk getting hurt like that again by him. *Nope. Nuh-uh.* I'd rather have a do-over of my face getting mangled—it would hurt less.

"I think you're going to have to accept the truth, Max. We. Are. Over. I am marrying Patricio."

"No. You won't."

"Says who?" I asked.

"Me."

I laughed.

He squeezed my shoulders firmly. "I know you, Lily. I know the smell of your darkest fears and the sound of your happiest laugh. I know how your heart beats faster when I kiss that little spot at the base of your neck." He leaned down to whisper in my ear, "And I know how your pussy feels when you can't get enough of my hard cock."

I jerked back and stared into his hazel eyes, unable to deny a single shocking word. "Your point?"

He slid his hand behind the back of my head and kissed me hard. His lips were punishing. His tongue was hot. His body told me he was ready for war and taking no prisoners.

Goddammit! I missed his soft lips. They felt like perfection against my mouth.

He pulled back, leaving me breathless. "My point, Lily, is that I own you. Not because I'm a possessive asshole, but because you already gave yourself to me."

He was overlooking how he'd turned me away when I groveled at his perfect feet and begged for forgiveness. *I have suffered and suffered and suffered some more. I'm done suffering.* I was not about to invite that horrific breed of vulnerability into my life. *Never again.*

I walked out of the back room and weaved my way between my display tables to the front door.

Max followed closely behind. "Where do you think you're going?"

I pushed the door open and stepped to the

side. "This is the only thing I've got to offer, Max. The exit. And don't come back."

He smiled, walked straight for me, and stopped with less than a foot between us. "You're mine, Lily, and you can pretend otherwise, but it won't change the fact: Patricio doesn't love you like I do and he never will."

I held up my left hand to show my engagement ring. "He says otherwise. And so do I."

Max shook his head. "Marketing, Lily. It's all about marketing." He turned and left, leaving my mind to wonder what he'd meant.

chapter two

I spent the rest of the day with the fakest smile I'd ever worn, a necessity to greet my handful of customers and make sales, but make no mistake, underneath that smile was outrage.

How dare he say that to me? Patricio loves me! Why else would a famous, hot-as-hell Italian actor want to marry me? Patricio had nothing to gain. Nothing. I mean, yes, marrying me would get him a green card, but with those big green eyes, that handsome face and sexy body, he could get anyone, really. Me, I came with baggage. I was complicated. I was not marriage-of-convenience material. *More like inconvenience material.* Besides, the studio had him on a work visa for some movie he was filming. He could eventually apply for a green card on his own.

Ha. See, Max! He does want me. Wait. What am I doing?

"Fuck!" I yelled, stomping my feet in the

back room, where I kept my inventory and had a desk for paperwork. I'd let Max get inside my head, which spoke to the deep emotional connection we'd once shared. A connection I'd released for sanity's sake.

I stared up at the industrial tiled ceiling, feeling like the Lily-planets were about to collide. *I am not letting this happen.* I had my life together now. *Okay. Sort of.* And I was happy now. *Sorta.* But Max was...he was...

"Gah!" I walked out to the floor, locked the front door, and turned the sign to closed before going for my broom. My cell vibrated in my pocket. I slid it out.

> **Patricio:** *Dinner at your place tonight? I will bring the salami.*

I smiled. Patricio loved to joke around and call his penis the salami. *So unlike Max.* Who was alpha male to the max. No pun intended. He was serious. Demanding. Always in control.

Christ. My smile melted away. I needed to tell Patricio what had happened today, and he would not be happy. He did not care for Maxwell Cole one little bit, and given that his ego rivaled Max's, he'd go into instant caveman mode. No, he'd never told me why the two weren't friends, but I guessed they'd had some sort of run-in at one of the many glamorous events both frequently attended. Over a woman? Maybe. But I didn't want to know.

My cell buzzed in my hand, reminding me of the unanswered text.

> **Me:** *Dinner sounds great. Looking forward to the cannoli.*

I grinned. At this very moment, Patricio was somewhere in L.A., swearing in Italian. No one, and I mean no one made fun of his junk.

> **Patricio:** *there will be spanking tonight*

"Yeah. You wish," I muttered to myself. We were not going to be having sex tonight. He would be too angry about Max's reemergence. And I had Max on the brain.

∾ ∾

Around eight fifteen, the front door to my little apartment buzzed, jarring me from my calming breathing exercises on the couch in my living room.

After the car accident, I had terrible nightmares followed by moments of sheer panic—a tightening in my stomach, dizziness, cold sweats. I endured a month of that before my mom talked me into seeing a therapist, Clara Monroe, who told me I suffered from a sort of post-traumatic stress. She taught me how to breathe and meditate, which helped a lot, but more importantly she convinced me to finally begin confronting my issues. Plainly put, growing up severely ugly had severely screwed with my head. I walked around with my chin held high, feeling confident and powerful, while a part of me, buried deep inside like a cancer, constantly whispered I wasn't good enough. "Try harder. You know they think you're a loser because you're ugly." "Run longer, because you're too fat." "Change your clothes. You look like shit in that outfit."

Ugh. That voice.

That motherfucking voice.

It was always there, telling me why I sucked. Why couldn't I have a voice that told me things like, "You're smart, you have an amazing heart, and be proud of who you are"?

"That's what mothers are for," Clara had said.

"Fine. Then put her in my head."

Clara had laughed. "If my mother were inside my head, I'd be in a padded cell. Not here with you."

"Good point."

But Clara had pointed out that fighting with myself—getting angry because I had this fugly voice in my head—was simply another form of self-hate. "The only way to break the cycle is to acknowledge it's there," she'd said.

"And then?"

She'd shrugged. "Make peace with it."

"How the hell do I do that?" I wanted to shoot the little bastard.

"You may not realize it, but the part of you that feels so imperfect has gotten you where you are. It's pushed you to be a better person. So has that part of you that says you're good and deserve good things."

Okay. Sure. I understood how not feeling perfect drove me to get into Stanford, pull straight A's, and become a workaholic—but it also kept me from having a peaceful, fulfilling life. Don't get me wrong. Most of the time, I felt good about myself. I worked hard, cared about others, and tried to do good. That was the real me. But that ugly whisper of self-doubt held me back sometimes, and I knew it. My relationship with Max being the perfect example. Some woman, who had a huge and very personal bone to pick with Max, had written a book that would expose his disorder to the world. She wanted me to corroborate her story, claiming that Max only planned to use me as proof that he did not have any such disorder. I mean, why would the world's hottest bachelor, a guy who couldn't stand the sight of ugly women, date someone like me, right? My heart had known that to be a lie, but my fugly little voice convinced me otherwise. I helped that horrible woman out Max and his secret, and the price had been catastrophic. The CEO of Cole Cosmetics, a company that had built its reputation on telling women that looks didn't matter and their beauty was "soul deep," actually couldn't handle being in the same room with an ugly woman. The optics were devastating. Of course, Max, true to his fearless nature, confronted the media head-on. He admitted to having his phobia and explained that while he'd kept it hidden, he'd refused to allow it to rule his life. He'd also confessed to being madly in love with me and proceeded to berate the press for their cruel comments about my looks.

Anyway, that all happened immediately after my accident. Once I'd heard about it and learned the real truth about his feelings for me, I came out and publicly apologized. Profusely. But it had been too late. CC's value had already tanked, and the press preferred to focus on bashing Max.

By the time I had the courage to see him and tell him how sorry I was, it was also too late. Or, at least, I thought so. Now I understood that Max hadn't thrown in the towel on us. He'd needed time to sort some things out, perhaps. As for me, the event made me realize how much work I needed to do on myself.

I stood from my couch to greet Patricio and smoothed down the front of my blue floral dress—a number with a cinched waist and pleated skirt from my boutique.

I went for the door, opened it, and gasped at the tall, stunningly handsome figure darkening my doorstep.

"Max? What are you doing here?"

He held out a dozen red roses, shoved them into my chest unceremoniously, and then peeked inside. "This your place?" His expression held a tinge of disgust.

I took the flowers begrudgingly. "Yes, this is my place, and before you say anything, it's what I can afford, including the thrift-store furniture you're about to call horrible." For the record, it wasn't horrible. Khaki sofa and armchair, plain natural wood coffee table, a round kitchen table in the eating area, and a few paintings of lilies on the wall. Simple, clean, modest. Affordable.

He stepped past me into the living room area, surveying the furniture with abhorrence. "I prefer the word disgraceful. You can do better."

"I have to put what I make into the store, not into furniture I barely use." I shut the door behind him and set the flowers down on the kitchen/dining table. I couldn't help checking him out as he continued looking around the room. Black jeans to accent his firm round ass, blue V-neck sweater, black leather jacket, his hair a fuck of a mess. *God, he looks so beautiful. And yet...I still want to kick him in his beautiful gonads.*

Just like old times.

"What about the settlement?" he asked.

He referred to the fact that I'd been awarded half a million dollars in damages because of my accident. I had nothing to do with suing the news station, but Max had seen to it that they'd paid. About forty percent had been taken by the government, twenty went to pay off my student loans from Stanford, and the other forty had gone into opening the store.

"Max? What do you want?" *Besides torturing me.* I could hardly look at him without wanting him or second-guessing my decision to turn him down.

"Can I sit?"

"No, you cannot sit," I replied. "Patricio is coming over."

Max narrowed his beautiful hazel eyes. "Wedding planning, I presume?"

"I haven't given him my answer yet."

"Why not?"

"Max, what do you want?"

"I have a business proposal."

He couldn't be serious. Those were the words he'd used when we began the journey that would forever change who we were. "No, Max. No proposals. You need to leave."

"I am going to start a new cosmetics company. And I'd like you to be the face. And my partner."

I jerked my head back. "Max," I said in a tone to indicate that I thought he'd lost his fucking head.

"Lily," he replied, as if to say "look at what I'm offering you."

"Max, what the hell are you trying to do?"

"As you're aware, I sold Cole Cosmetics. I've been investing in various companies, but I'd like to invest in you."

My mouth sort of flapped open and shut repeatedly.

He went on, "You've got a knack for connecting with people on a very genuine level. And you have a clear vision of what women want."

"What's that?"

He gave me a look.

Okay, I knew the answer to that: we didn't want companies to make us feel ugly just so they could make a profit. We wanted these marketing monsters to stop infecting us with these unattainable images of perfection. We deserved to love ourselves. As for marketing,

Max was the master of selling products on the basis of being good to one's self. In other words, "Pamper yourself! You deserve it!" instead of, "Hey. You're kind of ugly, but if you buy our product, you'll feel better about it." Nevertheless, Max's proposal was insane.

"I hate to point out the obvious," I said, "but you had a company that focused on real women. You sort of lost your credibility when you came out of the ugly-hater closet."

Max's eyes flicked with irritation.

"Sorry. But it's true."

He bobbed his head. "All right. Fine. But you've only proven why I need you. You'll be the face of the company, and you'll run it."

Wow. Max wanted to play hardball with my heart. He knew running a big company like that—one with a mission to change an industry with a severe moral deficit—had been my lifelong dream. It was why I'd gone to work for him. I'd wanted to learn the ropes from the marketing master.

My mind quickly do-si-doed around several flowery visions, complete with frolicking chipmunks and multicolored butterflies, of the two of us working side by side, changing the world one tube of eco-friendly lipstick at a time.

Stop. No. You can't go there. I couldn't do that and be with Patricio. There was too much baggage and temptation with Max.

"It's a kind thought, but I can't accept." I reached for the door handle to show him out.

"Why?"

The truth was too difficult to say, and frankly, all I wanted was to put him and me in the past. I needed to move on for sanity's sake. "I don't want to talk about this, Max."

He sat down on my sofa and looked up at me with those angry hazel eyes. "Too bad."

"Don't do this. Please."

"What?" He crossed his arms and leaned back.

"Don't push me to emotionally crack open for you."

"I'm asking you a simple question, Lily. Don't make it into more."

Damn him. So stubborn. I walked over, sat, and placed my hand over his. "You want me to beg again? I'm begging you. Please leave."

He dipped his head, giving me a look. He wasn't going to go until I gave him an answer.

"Fine. You want to hear the truth? It's because we are toxic together." Two uglies did not make a beautiful. We only made more ugly.

"Bullshit. You love me, Lily. I know you do. And if it's not enough for you, I accept that. But I love you and won't allow you to throw your life away on a business you don't really want and a man who's not your equal. At least this way, I'm saving you from one of those, and when you wake up with regards to Patricio, I won't be far."

"Goddammit." I leaned forward and pushed the heels of my palms against my eyelids, forgetting I'd put on heavy eye makeup to look extra nice for Patricio this evening. I'd even taken the time to curl my long blonde hair into sexy ringlets. A waste of time if Max didn't leave before Patricio arrived because he'd only focus on his nemesis being in my apartment. "You're impossible."

"Don't forget handsome as fuck, wealthy, and an excellent judge of character."

"You forgot arrogant."

"That's implied. Yes or no, Lily?"

Business partners? He was mad. "The answer is no. I'm happy with my little store, and it helps women in need."

Max let out a haughty laugh. "You and I both know you're capable of so much more, and if you take my offer, you'd find yourself in a position to help more than a few woman-owned micro-businesses."

Dammit. Dammit. Dammit! Max was such a good salesman. He always knew the angles.

"I see you still have the touch, selling ice to the Eskimos," I said.

His eyes narrowed. "And I see you're still shrinking back, Lily. From day one I was honest with you—you talk, but you don't walk."

"What the hell does that mean?"

"You may have had surgery to make your face beautiful, but you're still walking around like you don't deserve more in life."

"Why would you say that?" I snapped. It hurt. And it wasn't true. Okay, maybe it was, but everyone—*everyone*—had challenges to deal with. My fugly voice was mine, and I was dealing with it.

"You," he snarled, "are the smartest, most fucking tenacious woman I've ever met. You have gone after everything you've ever wanted with a ferocious hunger."

"Which is what I'm doing right now."

"A fucking boutique with crafty handmade clothes and shitty little humanitarian trinkets? And then there's the bonus of it sounding like your monthly bill. Exactly what were you thinking when you named it Lily's Pad?"

My jaw dropped.

"You know I'm saying the truth. You're selling yourself short again exactly like you did the first day you walked into Cole Cosmetics and applied for a job you were overqualified for. Your dream is to own your own cosmetics company. You were on a mission, and you wouldn't allow even an asshole like me to get in your way. That being said, you are no marketing expert—Ms. Lily Pad—but I sure the fuck am."

I felt that irresistible tugging, drawing me toward him. He had this way of knocking a person down to earth and then making them believe they could reach the stars, but only if they followed him because only he knew the way.

No. No. No! I'm not falling for it. "I owe my marriage with Patricio a fair chance. He won't get that with you around."

"Because you know that no one will ever love you like I do," he said matter-of-factly.

Dammit. His words were like thumbscrews. Only on my heart. *Heart screws?*

"Gah!" I threw up my hands. "He'll feel threatened. You're my ex-boyfriend. And you're not just any guy. You're Maxwell Cole."

He smiled. "Meaning you find me extremely attractive. Thank you. But if Patricio's insecure, that's not my fucking problem. Because this has nothing to do with him—this is business. And it's your future."

Liar, liar, pants on fire. "Max, I'm not going to work for you again."

"Not 'for.' Side by side. And don't be an idiot. This is an offer of a lifetime."

"Out. Now." I stood and pointed toward the door.

"Not until you say yes."

"No." I would, however, say yes to kicking

him in the ass.

Max rose from the couch, stood in front of me, and beamed down at my face, a reminder of how good it felt when he looked at me that way. Lust, love, affection—whatever. There was no bigger high than being adored by him.

"You're smart, Lily," he said with sincerity. "So I know you will be thinking it over. And then you'll come to realize you barely know Patricio. I've known him for years."

"Really?" I put my hand on my hip. "So you two were besties? Like sleepovers and secret handshakes?"

"You and your smart mouth need to listen." He shook his head disapprovingly. "Patricio is shallow. He can't challenge you like you need. He's lived a perfect life and will never understand you."

"Like you can?" I said bitterly.

"Yes. Absolutely. But that's beside the point. Sooner or later you're going to see I'm telling the truth. So go ahead and marry the guy. But he'll screw you over, and you'll be left with nothing but a failed business, debt, and a résumé you can't use. I'm offering you real love, happiness, and a chance to live your dream—I've thought of little else these past six months."

It didn't seem that way to me, since I hadn't heard a peep from the man. Nevertheless…*Sonofabitch! He is so damned good at selling!* It really pissed me off. The little crack about my résumé, for example? Let's just say that my name and face were fairly well known at this point. Tabloid after tabloid, reporter after reporter, my little affair with Max had gone global and landed me the nickname of the "billionaire breaker." The media had been fascinated with me, Max, and our story. And not in a nice way. No one could understand how one of the sexiest men on the planet could love me. Okay. Yes. I'll shut the hell up, because honestly, I hadn't been able to either. Anyway, despite my Ivy League résumé, no self-respecting company would ever hire me now.

"You always know the perfect angle to persuade people, Max," I growled, not meaning it as a compliment.

"It's a gift." He shrugged. "So did I succeed?"

"No. And now that I've heard what you had to say, it's time to go." I opened the door to show him out.

Max headed for the door, shaking his head. He wasn't thrilled about my turning him down this morning, and he wasn't thrilled now. I wasn't thrilled about looking at his perfect ass and towering lean frame with muscles in all the right places as he walked out. Everything about him undid me.

"Bye, Max. And…"

He turned to face me, and those hazel eyes—filled with frustration—created a vacuum in my head. All I could think about was how much I missed him.

I gulped, feeling my heart do a little wave action.

"Yes?" he said.

"Ummm…*thank you.* For caring so much about what happens to me." It felt wrong to end things on such an angry note even if I felt angry. Because despite everything, Max held a special place in my heart, and I knew he was doing all this because he cared.

He tilted his head to one side and stepped forward, speaking softly and gazing down at me as if I were his most cherished possession. "I only want to see you live a happy, successful life, like you deserve, Lily. So promise you'll think about what I said."

God, he was so good at getting to me.

I sighed quietly. "Fine. I'll think about it." I would also think about the fact that he'd popped into my life and asked me to marry him this morning—something I still couldn't persuade my brain cells to absorb.

Max stepped forward, reached out his hand, and traced the scar along my forehead. I knew what he was doing. He wanted to desensitize himself. Or maybe show me how far he'd come. Once upon a time, we couldn't be in the same room without him breaking into a sweat.

I watched with fascination while his perfect face—straight nose, full lips, and angular jaw—focused on me. I breathed in his expensive cologne and savored the memories it brought—him holding me close, making love to me, breathing against my neck. Max had been my first kiss, my first everything.

Caught up in the sensual memories, I closed my eyes, wishing that things had turned out differently. Why had I not believed in us? Okay, dammit. I knew why.

Suddenly, I felt his lips on mine. Soft, hot, and sensual. He felt so good, so right. Gentle and strong all rolled into one.

"Lily!" Patricio's voice roared.

I pushed back from Max and turned my head. Patricio stood ten feet away. Rage sizzled in his bright green eyes.

"You fucking bastard." Patricio zeroed in on Max and ran straight for him.

chapter three

Well, that's something I never thought I'd see. With my mouth hanging open, I watched two completely hot men tumble around on the sidewalk in front of my first-floor apartment, trying to beat the crap out of each other.

Yes, I did understand that the proper reaction would be to panic or feel angered by their immature behavior, but I wasn't just anyone. Remember, I was once the girl no one looked at except with pity or disgust. Yes, I compensated with my personality and still had lots of girlfriends, but getting male attention felt alien, and this was no exception. Italy's hottest actor and America's sexiest bachelor were fighting over me.

This is definitely strange. And so amazingly hot. Wait. Am I evil for thinking that?

Max, a slightly larger man, rolled over Patricio and cocked his fist. Patricio threw up his arm and crosscut Max in the jaw, sending him back. Patricio took advantage of the opportunity and scrambled forward, straddling Max.

As Patricio pulled back his fist, aiming for Max's perfect nose, I screamed, "No!"

Max thrust his knee upward and launched Patricio forward. Patricio's fist pummeled the cement below.

Ouch. That had to hurt.

Patricio wailed.

Yep. It hurt.

"You fucking asshole. You don't deserve her!" Max twisted his body and threw Patricio down, landing a punch straight on Patricio's cheekbone.

Blood began running from a cut on Patricio's face, which immediately jolted me out of my shock and into the worst panic ever. They really wanted to kill each other.

"Okay. That's enough!" I barked, doing an awkward little waving action with my hands. "Stop. Both of you."

Max and Patricio rolled and grunted, each one trying to get the upper hand.

"Stop! Goddammit!" I tried to grab for an arm to pull them apart, but they were like two feral cats, moving so fast I couldn't see who was who or what was what.

From the corner of my eye, I caught a neighbor taking pictures through her window.

And goodie. We'll be getting tabloid coverage.

Flustered, I stared down at the two beautiful jackasses and gushed out a breath. *Imbeciles.* Fighting resolved nothing.

"Stop!" I yelled. "That's it! That's fucking it."

Their tangled limbs and grunting bodies rolled toward me, knocking me to the ground. I fell back, landing with a hard thump on the cement, and hit my elbow to break the fall.

"Fuck!" I groaned and rolled to the side, cupping my elbow.

They didn't take notice or seem to give one freaking dingle berry about little ol' me. The bozos continued tumbling around like two schoolboys fighting on the playground.

I peeled myself off the walkway, got to my feet, and rubbed my throbbing arm. *Wow. Just wow.* They really couldn't care less about me.

I threw up my hands—*Ouch! My elbow*—and threw them down. "Fine! You know what?" I yelled. "Fucking kill each other!"

I marched past them, slammed my door shut, turned the dead bolt, and went into my bedroom. The knocking began immediately, but I was not about to answer. Let them have their awesome macho-man contest. Yes, Patricio had a right to be angry, but he should be upset with me. Me! I'd let Max kiss me. And it was wrong. I knew that.

Of course, Max had crossed the line by

kissing me, so I got to be angry with him for that. He knew exactly how to work me.

After two minutes, the knocking ceased and my phone beeped. *So now they're texting me?* I walked into the living room, grabbed my phone, and shut it off. They could stew tonight. Both of them. And maybe, just maybe, in the morning, I might be coolheaded enough to talk to them. But not now. At this moment, my damned elbow hurt and I needed to process what had happened. After I completed my angry spinning, of course.

I went to my small kitchen, popped open the freezer, and grabbed the blue plastic ice block I used for my lunches. I wrapped it in a towel and held it to the back of my arm.

The loud knocking started again. "Seriously?" I scowled. "You two need to take a hint." I marched over, unlocked the dead bolt, and jerked the door open. "Screw you! Okay! I don't want…" my voice trailed off as a news crew shoved a microphone in my face.

"Miss Snow! What can you tell us about the fight between Maxwell Cole and Patricio Ferrari? Were they fighting over you? Is it true one hit you? Who threw the punch? Will you be pressing charges?"

What the hell? How had the news crew come so fast?

My mouth flapped for several moments

before I slammed the door shut and pushed my back against the door. "No, no, no." The chaos was starting all over again.

This is all Max's fault. I had to get rid of him.

After a very restless night with a very sore arm, I threw in the towel on the whole sleep idea and decided to go for an early morning run on the beach, aka my therapy because it usually cleared my head. There was something energizing about seeing the wide-open ocean right before sunrise when the air felt crisp and crackled with the possibilities of a new day.

So after putting on my blue running shorts and white sports tank and placing my arm into a little sling made from a scarf, I ran north for an hour until the sun came up.

My body tired with sweat, I plunked down in the cool sand with my legs stretched out. I wanted to stay there all day, staring at the calming ocean, because when my thoughts returned to my shop, my life, Patricio and Max, everything felt so damned heavy.

"Whatcha looking at?" said a deep voice.

I swiveled my head to find Max—shirtless, broad chest heaving, tatt-covered upper arms flexing with muscles—wearing only running shoes and black shorts. His lightly tanned, sculpted abs and pecs glistened with sweat, making my heart beat a little faster.

Okay. A lot faster.

Interesting fact: Max's magnificent body was also a byproduct of his dysfunctional brain, which drove him to relentlessly pursue perfection in all things. The bedroom was no exception. When we'd been together, he'd used that lean, chiseled body and large cock of his to work me over repeatedly. He knew exactly how to move inside me—the timing and pressure of his thrusts, the grinding against my c-spot, the pace of his hot kisses. I'd now been with one other man—Patricio—but he didn't compare. And part of me believed no one ever would.

But there's more to a relationship than mind-blowing sex. Friendship, for example. Friendship is—

My eyes stuck to Max's chest. *Damn, he's ripped.* Max had added some extra definition to those chiseled abs. He looked amazing.

Oh, stop.

"What are you doing here?" I asked.

"You love to run. I love to run. I guess we decided to do it at the same time."

I lifted a brow. His home was in north Chicago, so my hunch told me he was staying at one of the five-star resorts in town. None of them were anywhere near this beach. "At the same location, too?"

Max didn't answer. Instead, he sat next to me in the moist sand and stared out at the ocean. "I'm not sorry about last night," he said flatly.

I shook my head. "You should be." I pointed to my sling. My elbow was black and blue and swollen.

Max looked at my arm. "What happened?"

I huffed. "Of course, you don't remember because you were too busy fighting Patricio."

"He attacked me."

"Yes, but you kissed me."

"I won't apologize for that." Max looked forward, watching a breaking wave. "But I am sorry about your arm, even if it was Patricio's fault."

God. He was so damned...stubborn! Of course, it was what I loved about him, too. His iron will. That being said, "I have to go." I hopped up and started walking back.

"Lily, wait." Max got to his feet, grabbed my good arm, and stopped me. "Did you think about my offer?"

"What? No! I was too busy getting knocked over by you two and fending off the press at my front door. Thank you for that, by the way."

"I texted you a warning when I left. Didn't you see it?"

"No. I didn't see it."

He shrugged his dark brows as if to say: "Not my problem. Next time check your texts." But instead he said, "Am I the only person who found it odd that the paparazzi happened to be in the neighborhood to film us?"

"You're not implying that Patricio had something to do with it? Because he had no clue you were going to be there."

Max shrugged. "Perhaps he was hoping they'd be there to capture your big yes to his marriage proposal."

I scoffed. "That's ridiculous. He wouldn't do that." Would he?

"The man will do anything to advance his career, and getting free publicity is no exception."

"If that were true, then Patricio and I would've had our pictures popping up in the tabloids every time we went…" My voice faded as I realized there had been a few occasions where we were surprised by photographers. The last time was at a new sushi restaurant he'd taken me to near Malibu.

I'm sure those were coincidences. Weren't they? Wait…

"You know what? I don't have time for this. I have a store to open." I turned away, but Max grabbed my arm again.

"Lily," he growled, "you didn't give me an answer about my business proposal."

"No. I don't want to go into business with you. There. You have your answer."

"Then you need more time to think it over, just like you need to reconsider my marriage proposal."

"What are you doing, Max?"

He didn't answer my question. Instead he said, "I stayed up all night thinking about how that kiss last night proved you don't love him. Otherwise you would've resisted. So tell me why you insist on marrying him, Lily. And then I'll leave if you want. You'll never see me again."

I took a breath. "It's exactly what I told you last night. We're bad for each other."

"I happen to disagree. You helped me when no one else could. And I helped you see your true potential. We're not simply good for each other, we're perfect. And we need each other."

"What you *need* is a woman who will never doubt you and be there to stroke your massive ego."

"No. You're wrong again. I need someone who tells it like it is. You."

I placed my hands on my waist and shook my head at my running shoes. He was making this so hard. "I'm fucked up, Max. And will always doubt you love me because despite my improved looks, I still feel like that girl who stood in your office eight months ago, asking for a job, but all you saw was her face—a face that revolted you."

Max's jaw tightened. My words clearly angered him.

I went on, "And can you honestly tell me you won't relapse? Or that if we did get married that you wouldn't repeat your mother's mistakes? What if we had kids? Did you think about that? Because chances are, any child of mine will not come out looking like a beauty queen." It was a harsh thing to say. I knew that. Just like I knew any child of mine would be absolutely beautiful to me and insanely loved. But Max needed to understand that our future didn't look promising. "Max, can you honestly say you wouldn't force our child to have a nose job at thirteen or punish it for being imperfect." It was what his mother had done to him.

He shook his head from side to side. "I would never..." But I heard doubt in his voice. Or maybe it was fear.

"I can't risk it," I said. "I can't risk loving you and then having a family simply to see if maybe, *maybe* you'll love your son or daughter like my parents loved me." And I certainly couldn't risk opening my heart to him again. The pain of our breakup still made me feel sick when I thought about it.

Max looked down at the sand. He understood my point. He could say that he loved me all day long, but he could not guarantee that he'd always be there for me and our children like we deserved. Simply put, the depths of his fuckedupness were unknown.

I waited for him to respond, but he looked away. His brow beaded with fresh sweat.

Christ. See, I'm right. Whatever images or thoughts were going through his head freaked him the hell out. Maybe he'd imagined holding an ugly baby.

His head abruptly snapped up. "No. I'm not letting you throw us away based on what-ifs. I *do* know, Lily. I *know* who I am. I know the kind of man I am. And I know that I would never abandon you. I'd stick by my children, too, regardless of my struggles."

And there it was. The point.

I grabbed his arm and squeezed gently. "Listen to yourself. Having a life with me shouldn't be a struggle. It shouldn't be an act of loyalty or duty or a form of torture. It should be the one thing that makes you hop out of bed in the morning with a giant smile. I can't give you that. And I could never be happy knowing that maybe on the inside, you don't love me or them like they deserve." It was so surreal having a conversation about children who didn't exist yet. Especially, because in my heart, I felt like I was letting real people go, because I was letting him go.

Max's dark brows furrowed, his lips flattened, and his jaw muscles ticked. He did not like being told no, but he definitely didn't like hearing that I didn't have faith in him as a future father.

"I'm sorry, Max. But you wanted the truth, and now you have it. We're not good for each other." I still had a lot of healing and growing to do to accept myself, but being with Max wouldn't allow it. I'd always be focusing on him and his phobia, wondering and worrying and doubting him or doubting us. Not healthy. It had taken these past six months to realize it, but I saw that now.

Max blew out a long breath and crossed his arms over his chest. "I can't believe I'm about to say this, but maybe you're right. I will struggle. I will fight. But I've yet to fail at anything. And I know you will never find a man willing to work harder to make you happy. But you? You've given up. Not simply on your career, but on your life. So you don't believe we could work? All right. There's nothing I can do about it. But trust me, Lily. I know the man. He's not the one for you."

I stared up at Max. *Okay, he knows something. He has to.* There was too much conviction in his voice. "Why do you keep saying that?"

Max scratched his chin and looked away.

"Max," I urged him.

He shook his head. "Some things are better left alone."

Now it was my turn to shake my head. "You can't do that."

"Do what?"

"Ask for complete honesty from me and not reciprocate."

"I'm Maxwell Cole. I can do anything I like."

I tilted my head. "You think this is funny?"

"No. I think you need to trust me, and if history has taught you anything, it should be that."

Low blow.

"Max, please. Tell me why you think Patricio and I won't work."

"Besides the fact that he's not me and will never understand you like I do?"

I rolled my eyes. "Just tell me."

Max grumbled under his breath. "Why don't you ask him? He is going to be your fiancé. Perhaps the honesty should begin there."

Jerk. "Fine. I will. Unlike you, I'm sure he'll have the balls to tell me. Now, if you don't mind, I have a business to run." I turned away, took a step, and fell over.

"Lily!"

chapter four

When I came to with a nauseous churning in my stomach and a light head, Max held me in his strong—so, so strong—arms and carried me down the beach, my cheek pressed to his chest.

"What happened? Put me down," I mumbled.

"No. Something's wrong with you."

"I'm fine—I'm just tired." The long days at the store, the stress of my business failing, and the restless nights had finally caught up with me.

"If passing out means you're tired, then it's all the more reason to rethink your business strategy."

Max cut inland and headed for a very tall set of wooden stairs to get us over the sandbank.

"Where are we going?" I asked, my legs bouncing as he huffed and moved at a quick pace.

"Callahan is waiting in the parking lot."

"You brought your chauffeur to Santa Barbara?"

"Where I go, he goes."

"And you are going to...?" He'd promised he'd leave once I told him the truth about why we couldn't be together.

"To the hospital."

"No. I'm fine. It's happened before. Please put me down."

He gave me a stern look and lowered me to my feet.

I pressed my palms to my knees, holding my body in the doubled-over position to get my bearings. "I forgot to eat last night." Now that I thought about it, I hadn't eaten since yesterday morning. I didn't usually do that, but with Max showing up and the fight and everything else, the emotions had killed my hunger. "You can go now. I'll be fine once I eat."

He placed his strong hand between my shoulder blades and made circles. "I'm taking you home."

Oh, God. His touch felt so damned good. "No. Just go."

"You're being ridiculous. My driver is waiting up in the parking lot."

I glanced at the long stretch of beach standing between me and my home and then at the flight of wooden stairs leading up to the public lot. "You'll have to help me up the stairs."

"No problem." Without warning, he grabbed my arm and effortlessly whipped me over his shoulder. With my five-six height and slender frame, a guy like Max—six three, muscles in all the right places—could lift me easily, but he made a big show of it.

I'm a dude. A big strong dude. You know you're impressed. Grunt, grunt.

"Max!"

"What?" He marched up the stairs with a smug bounce in his step.

He's totally enjoying this! He'd thrown me over his shoulder on the night he'd taken me up to his bedroom at his home near Chicago. He'd fucked me senseless that night. He'd fucked me senseless the next day, too. Oh, hell. It had been the best weekend of my life.

Our sextastic weekend.

He had to know that carrying me brought back very sexual memories. Hot, sensual, orgasmic memories that included his tongue licking its way up my inner thigh, his hands pinching my nipples, his thick cock hammering me from behind.

Oh God. No. No. No. You're not getting horny. You're simply remembering how good he felt sliding between your legs. So, so hard. So, so good.

I shook it off quickly.

"Put me down, Max." My body bounced on

his shoulder. It wasn't the most comfortable of positions and wasn't helping my light-headedness.

"Stop whining, Lily." He gave my ass a hard slap and the sting sent an instantaneous, scorching arousal between my legs. I wasn't into pain, but he'd slapped my ass on that special night in his bedroom. I would never forget the sting that initiated the most erotic weekend of my life.

I gritted my teeth and pushed my lids together nice and tight. This was exactly my point. I couldn't be around Max and not...not...want him. But I didn't want to be one of those stupid girls who knew a relationship was completely doomed, but jumped in anyway, only to whine like an idiot after it all went south.

Finally at the top, Max tilted forward and slid me off.

Gripping my shoulders, he looked down at me and flashed a cocky smile. Oh yes. He knew exactly what he was doing.

"That was dirty, Max."

He looked over my shoulder, ignoring my comment. "There's Callahan. Shall we?" He held out his elbow.

I marched ahead, unable to look at him. I was so goddamned turned on, but my heart didn't want this. It didn't want to play this game any longer.

chapter five

The ride back to my "unacceptable apartment," as Max called it, took only a few minutes, but as far as my body was concerned, it felt like an eternity of sexual torture. Thankfully, Max had put on a black T-shirt to cover those drool-provoking washboard abs, but the smell of his expensive cologne and fresh sweat permeated the car, only fueling the intimate memories with my ex-boss.

As I prepared to deliver a very firm goodbye-for-forever speech, the town car pulled up to the curb in front of my complex—a two-story, 1960s Spanish-style building with a red tile roof, white stucco exterior, and arched windows and doorways. Max's expression turned from serious to surprised.

My gaze followed the direction of his stare through the windshield. "Crap." *They* were back. Only this time, instead of one news crew, there were six.

"What the hell is going on?" I groaned. Didn't they have wars and election email scandals to report on?

"Hmmm...this is unfortunate." Max grinned as if he'd won some giant victory. "I guess you'll have to come back to my hotel."

"Nice try."

"Only trying to help," he said with smug amusement.

"If you want to help, how about staying away?" The reporters wanted him or Patricio, not me. "All of my clothes are inside, and I have to open the shop in forty minutes."

Max's smile melted away.

"What?" I asked.

"Something doesn't feel right."

"No kidding. I have a mob of reporters stalking my home." *Well, screw them!* I had nothing to be ashamed of and that included my scars, my love life, or my past.

I pulled the handle of the car door, and Max tugged me back by the shoulder. "Wait. Let me deal with them. They'll probably go away if I give them a statement." He slid out of his side of the car.

Mr. Fearless. Seriously, aside from his little "issue," nothing scared the man. It was very hot.

I watched Max's lean, tall frame make confident strides towards the pack of wolves, who immediately spotted him and swarmed. I could only see the top of his head from my vantage point, but it struck me as odd that he stood there for all of five seconds before returning to the car with the reporters on his heels.

He opened the door and slid inside. "Drive," he ordered Callahan, who obeyed without question.

"What's going on?" My racing heart told me I was not going to like it.

Max's dark brows shrugged, and he let out a breath.

"What!" I demanded.

With a calmness that terrified me, he looked out the window. "I suggest you come back to the hotel with me." There wasn't an ounce of flirt, fun, or cockiness in his voice this time.

"Why? What happened?" I growled.

He slid his cell from his shorts pocket, tapped a few times on the screen, and handed it to me.

I took the phone in my hands and gazed at the image of Patricio naked, having sex with another woman.

"What?" I covered my mouth. "This can't be real."

"Let's get you somewhere private, and we'll figure it out together." Max reached out and placed his hand on my thigh. "I'm sorry, Lily. This isn't right."

As I would expect, Max had the most incredible bungalow at the most expensive hotel in town, the Four Seasons. Private pool and patio with outdoor fireplace, gorgeous furnishings, full living room and dining room. Quiet. Secluded. Perfect. So Max.

Not that I really cared at the moment because I literally felt sick to my stomach.

Max tossed his room key on the marble coffee table in the living room and gestured for me to sit on the sofa. My wobbly knees gave out as I lowered my trembling body onto the gold-embroidered seat cushion.

"Would you care for a scotch?" he said, heading straight for the bar in the corner.

Too frazzled to realize—or give a shit—that it was still breakfast time, I nodded and lay across the couch, crossing my arms over my face. "Fuuuck," I groaned. *Whyyy?* I'd been so ready to go all in with Patricio, knowing that we weren't banana-ape-shit-lust-crazy over each other, but that we had something solid. Friendship. And, yes, attraction. Patricio was a very handsome man—six two, an athletic body, olive skin, short brown hair, and bright green eyes. He was one hundred percent Italian in terms of his slightly longer nose, but it fit his cute face. He was also passionate and spontaneous. He loved his "big fat Italian family," whom he claimed couldn't wait to meet me.

Max sat down on the couch, using his firm ass to scoot my legs over. "Here. This will make you feel better."

I sat up and pushed my back against the armrest, placing my legs over Max's lap. Max held out a crystal tumbler full of golden brown liquid.

"Thanks." I took the glass and stared at the thing for a moment. "Why do you think he fucked her, Max?" As if being cheated on wasn't bad enough, Patricio had done it with Adeline Taylor—a very hot Hollywood actress who used to date Max. They'd ended things when Max fell in love with me. Needless to say, I had no affection for the woman. The few times our paths had crossed, she'd treated me like a mangy dog.

Max looked down at his own drink and pondered. "You know my answer, Lily. Why ask?"

"I want to hear you say it."

"All right, then. He fucked that woman because he's the true definition of a man-whore. It's exactly as I told you the night you met him: he'll fuck anything that moves."

I lifted my glass to my lips and nearly gagged from the smell. *Ick. I don't want this.* "Got anything else?" I needed something to numb the ache in my heart, but I'd forgotten how much I disliked scotch, aka cinnamon-infused gasoline.

Max's plump lips pulled to the side. "On second thought, you really should eat. Why don't I order you breakfast instead? You said you haven't eaten."

"Thanks, but I'm not hungry. I'll take an orange juice if you have any." If I ate anything now, I'd likely toss it up. My stomach was churning and knotting. *How could Patricio do this to me?*

Max stared for a moment with those sultry hazel eyes, his square jaw ticking. "But you'll need your strength for when I fuck you." He grinned and those two stubble-covered dimples puckered.

My mouth dropped open. Did he really think that my relationship catastrophe had magically cleared the way for him and me to fuck? Clearly, he had not listened to a word I'd said about why we were doomed.

Maybe he just wants to fuck. After all, he is a man. Dick first, feelings second. Or in Patricio's case: feelings never.

Max slid my feet from his lap and went to

get a small bottle of OJ from the minibar fridge. Meanwhile, I wished that mental Drano existed so I could wash away the image of Patricio lying naked between Adeline Taylor's legs, her red fingernails digging into his ass. They'd been fucking all right. No doubt about it. The other photos showed him naked, paddleboarding over turquoise water, with her sitting in front of him. I guessed they were in the US Virgin Islands because that was where he'd been "working" part of this past week.

Max returned with my drink, and I chugged it down.

He took the empty bottle from my hand and placed it on the coffee table before lifting my legs and sitting. He patted my shin. "Are you sure you won't let me order you some room service? I seem to remember you being a fan of pancakes."

"I'm really not hungry." I only wanted to cry. Just not in front of him. "God, I'm such an idiot," I said under my breath.

"No, Lily. It's what I've been trying to tell you. You. Are. Perfect. You simply aren't perfect for him. No one is."

"Thanks," I said unappreciatively.

"His being a cheating asshole truly has nothing to do with you. I wouldn't lie. Not to you."

I shook my head, feeling the orange juice

mix with my sour angry stomach. "But you *would* keep the truth from me."

Max took a moment, mulling something over. "Patricio's family and mine were once close. They vacationed on the French Riviera. We vacationed on the French Riviera. But then one year, when my sister, Mabel, turned sixteen, it all changed."

Uh-oh. I didn't like the sound of this.

He continued, "Let's just say that Patricio's acting career started early, and he honed his skills deceiving young women."

"He Mr. Wickhamed your sister?"

Max lifted a questioning brow.

"He played her," I clarified.

Max nodded. "She never told me the whole story, but it doesn't take much to imagine. She was devastated for months after he tossed her aside. Then she found out he'd slept with three of her friends, too."

What an asshole. By my calculations, Patricio was three years older than Mabel, Max's sister.

I inhaled through my nostrils, trying to digest it. So this was it—the reason Max hated Patricio. Still, it didn't explain why Patricio hated Max back.

"What did you do to him?" I asked.

Max took a long time to answer while he stared at something that stretched beyond present time. "I almost killed him."

I pulled back my head. I had *not* expected that.

Max nodded. "I found Patricio and beat him within an inch of his life. If it weren't for my family's money and their ability to settle things quietly, I probably would've gone to the French equivalent of juvie."

I almost had no words. It was one thing to play the protective brother, but it was another to almost kill someone.

"Keep in mind," he said, "I was only fifteen at the time and my mother had systematically stripped all joy from my life. My sister was the only thing I cared about."

My stomach churned again. It was so very strange to think of this beautiful, strong, confident man growing up in such a mentally fucked-up home. To his credit, he'd taken that pain and suffering and turned himself into something extraordinary.

"I'm so sorry, Max."

He laughed. "You had your heart broken by that piece of shit and you're telling *me* you're sorry?"

I shrugged. "I'll be okay. I've survived worse." I looked at him so he'd know what I meant.

"I'm sorry, Lily. I shouldn't have waited so long."

He referred to the six months. "Then why did you?"

He scratched his scruffy chin. "I realized that I'd built Cole Cosmetics out of sheer hatred for my mother. Which made me angry all over again. I thought I was free of her and was my own man, when really my entire world still revolved around that monster. Once I saw that, I needed time."

"To do what? More therapy?" I felt a spark of jealousy, picturing what that therapy might involve. Or more accurately stated, *who* it might involve. Had he found some other woman to spend his nights with to continue what he'd started with me? Had he fucked her, too?

He paused for a long moment. "It's a very long story—and now is not the right time to share it." He gave my knee a pat and then stood. "I'm going to order food and ask them to bring you clothes from their shop."

He walked over to the phone on the end table and dialed. Meanwhile, I stared at his back and broad shoulders. I couldn't help feel the need to touch him. And rub my naked body all over him. With his penis inside me. All right, sex. I wanted comfort sex.

"I'm going to take a shower." *A cold one.* I got off the couch and scurried to the bathroom. I closed the door and pressed my back to it, wincing. Honestly, I needed to get out of here, maybe go to my brother's apartment. My parents' house was not an option because my mother and father were serial worriers. They freaked out whenever I wasn't smiling. "What's wrong? Something's wrong. What *happened*?" My mother's face would turn pale and my father's would go red. I suspected their overprotective, worrying nature stemmed from feeling guilty that they'd brought me into the world with an extremely ugly face, making life a bit hard. As for my brother, he was born with a rare spinal deformation and was wheelchair bound, which still evoked heavy doses of daily worrying from my parents despite his very good health, intelligence, and capable body. He was Mr. Independence.

I slipped my cell from my pocket and dialed my brother to leave a message. He'd be at work right now, teaching math over at the elementary school. "Hey, John. It's me. Can you leave your house key for me at your front office? I need a place to hide today—a long and wonderful story I'll share with you later. Love you, bye." I hung up, feeling kind of green.

Okay. The orange juice had not been such a great idea. I scrambled for the toilet and threw up.

"Lily?" Max's voice projected from the now open doorway.

"Go away!" I swiped my hand through the air to shoo him out.

"This is the third time I've seen you get sick since I got here."

I groaned with my head over the toilet. "Go...I'm fine."

Max grumbled and left the bathroom. I pried myself from the floor, shut the door again, and started the shower, taking time to use the entire miniature bottle of complimentary mouthwash to remove the foul taste.

After rinsing the sweat from my morning run, my mind settled back to Patricio. I needed to call him. I needed to tell him what a piece of lying garbage he was. He had to know by now that I'd seen the photos.

I finished the shower, wrapped myself in a towel, and peeked out the door. "Do you have a robe I could borrow?"

Max stood next to the dining table, texting away with a huge frown on his face—lips in a hard line, brows pushed together.

"Max?"

He looked up and his eyes set on me and my towel-encased body. A lust-crazed yearning burned in his eyes.

"Max? Robe."

"My apologies. Seeing you all wet like that brings back very nice memories."

"I just threw up and my almost fiancé

cheated on me. Maybe you can put a hold on the sexual commentary."

Max stared for a moment. "Doubtful. Being near you makes me think about very sexual things."

I felt the same thing, too, which only made me more confused. How could I feel heartbroken over Patricio and lust after Max at the same time?

Max walked into the bedroom and brought out a fluffy white robe for me. "Here you go."

"Thanks." I grabbed it, closed the door, and then slid it on. I wrapped my long blonde hair in my towel and then went back out to await some clothing and a call or text back from my brother.

"So," Max said, watching me walk back over to the couch, "I had the hotel recommend a doctor nearby."

"I have a doctor." She'd been my physician since I was ten, and she'd already seen me a few times over the past months. I was stressed out and overworking myself. Plain and simple.

"Then you should make an appointment."

"I don't need to see her. I know exactly what's wrong with me." An unfaithful boyfriend and an ex I still burned for but couldn't, shouldn't, wouldn't be with.

Max stared for a moment and then, as if a switch flipped, he turned ice cold—rigid posture, emotional void in his stunning hazel eyes.

"What?"

He blinked. "Nothing."

"Why are you looking at me like that?"

"Like..." His eyes shifted from side to side. "What?"

"Like a unicorn landed on my head."

"I have no clue what you mean."

He's lying. I could see it on his face. I physically felt him withdraw from the room despite him still standing in front of me.

Before I could push him further, my phone beeped and the doorbell buzzed.

"Excuse me." Max turned away to answer, and I grabbed my cell from my pocket. It was a text from my brother.

> **John:** *The fucking asshole! I'll kill him.*
>
> **Me:** *Be my guest. Did you leave the key?*
>
> **John:** *I'm not letting anyone run you out of your home. I'll meet you at your place in ten.*

What? No. There were reporter-parasites waiting.

> **Me:** *Just leave me a key, and we'll catch up later.*

I waited for a reply, but it didn't come.

Me: *????*

Nothing.

"Dammit," I whispered.

Max appeared with two pairs of shorts—pink and black—and a few small T-shirts draped over his arm. "Sorry. They didn't have large."

I frowned with confusion. I was a size six. Today, I could possibly squeeze into a four. No, I wasn't obsessed with my weight, but I had a naturally thin frame and obsessed over running. Like I said, having the face of the elephant girl left me with few advantages to exploit: intelligence, personality, body, and hair.

"Those will do fine." I snagged the black tee and pink shorts and headed into the bathroom. I put on the clothes and emerged to find Max's driver standing in his black suit, hands clasped together.

"Uhh...where'd Max go?" I asked.

With the steely tone of a well-trained soldier, Callahan gave nothing away. "Mr. Cole had urgent business to attend to. He asked me to stay with you."

"Max left. And asked you to babysit me." *What in the world?*

Awkwardness tinged his brown eyes. Callahan was a plain man with thinning brown hair, a very thick build, and intimidating presence. Ex-military for sure. "No, ma'am. He simply requested I assist."

"Assist?" I folded my arms across my chest.

"Yes, ma'am." His Adam's apple bobbed. "If you should..." Bob, bob. "Need anything. Vitamins, for example."

Had Max lost his mind? "No. I don't need vitamins. But you can give me ride home."

Callahan's brown eyes flared open.

"What?" Everyone was behaving so strangely.

"I think Mr. Cole might prefer you stay here and await his return."

Oh. Well, in that case... "You can bring me home, or you can tell Mr. Cole I left on my own. Either way, I am leaving."

"Let me see you home, then." Callahan turned and opened the door.

"Thank you." Where the hell had Max gone in such a hurry? I would ask Callahan, but I already knew the man was paid for his discretion as much as for his speedy driving. And I wasn't about to let John deal with that mess in front of my apartment on his own. With my luck, one of the reporters would say something inflammatory and John would run them over with his wheelchair. After disemboweling them. No. John didn't fuck around. He was a hothead and couldn't care less if his legs didn't work because his arms worked just fine.

I grabbed my stuff and followed Max's chauffeur out the door, grabbing my cell to send Max a text. I punched in some very choice words but stopped. It felt reactionary and juvenile. The reason I really felt angry was because I needed him to be there for me, and he'd left. We'd been enemies—oh God, how I'd once hated him—we'd been boss and employee, and then we'd been lovers. But we'd never been friends. And that, somehow, felt more important to me than anything else right now.

Me: *Goodbye, Max.*

chapter six

Sitting in the back of Max's limo, I pulled up to my apartment for round two with the paparazzi, expecting them to have my brother surrounded.

Why must all of the men in my life be so hotheaded?

I exited the car without receiving more than a grunt from Callahan, who'd been like an ice sculpture the entire way. He did not show emotions like normal people.

I stomped toward my apartment and immediately spotted the slouching vultures on their smartphones, but no John.

Where is he? He should've beat me here.

The moment they saw me, they jumped to their feet and began throwing insults masked as questions. "Did Patricio Ferrari give you an STD? Did he dump you for Adeline Taylor yet? Did he ask you to *ménage*?"

I rolled my eyes, pushed my key into the

lock, and entered my apartment. There sat John, giving me a startle.

"Oh God." I placed my hand over my heart. "I thought I would find you outside, kicking the crap out of one of those guys."

John had brown eyes and blond hair—same as me—and was built big like my father, only bigger because he liked to play sports—basketball, swimming, skiing. There wasn't much he couldn't manage. He'd even been into rock climbing for a while, which drove my mother absolutely frantic. "What if you fall, John? Huh?"

"Oh no. I might end up in a wheelchair," he would reply with a smart-ass snort and then receive a smack on the back of the head from my father for being disrespectful.

I threw my keys on the coffee table and took a calming breath, wanting to address John in an even tone. I had zero desire to fight with him, but the angry steam had built up in my mental engine. One more lump of shitty coal and Lily's head would explode. "Is there a particular reason you left the school in the middle of the day and wouldn't allow me to hide at your place, my dear sweet brother?"

John wheeled in front of me. He had on his usual khaki pants and a blue golf shirt with the school logo, which allowed me to see the veins pulsing in his neck and biceps. He was pissed.

"Is there a particular reason you left your door unlocked when there's a mob outside trying to stalk you?"

"They weren't there this morning, and I guess I was distracted."

"I can guess why. And when I see him, I'm going to hunt that man-cunt down and dismember him."

Man-cunt? Well, there's a new one. "Whoa there, John. While I appreciate the enthusiasm you show for protecting me, I need to be clear. This is my life, and I will deal with it." I crossed my arms over my chest and looked down at my brother and his flaring nostrils.

"You're a Snow. And Snows stick together," he snarled.

Dear Lord. On a scale of one to ten, ten being a PMSing mother lion, my family was a twenty with the overprotectiveness. This was the one thing about them I considered both a blessing and a curse—mostly the latter.

"I let you manage your own love life, John. You need to allow me the space to deal with mine."

"Sorry. Doesn't work like that. The big-brother handbook dictates I must intervene."

Gah. What an ass. "Stop. Okay? You don't see me running around threatening to dismember your exes or calling them woman-dicks." The opposite of a man-cunt, of course.

He crossed his beefy arms over his chest. "That's because you're too busy trying to avoid confrontation by hiding in my apartment."

Ughhh... "I needed a quiet place to think, and I can't do it here with those dipshits outsi—" A loud knock on the door broke my concentration. "Dammit. Why can't they leave me alone?"

"Let me deal with them." John went to the front door and yanked it open, but it wasn't the tabloid vultures.

Max. I gasped, but why wasn't I surprised? He'd unexpectedly shown up three times in the last twenty-four hours.

Blocking the door, John scowled up at Max, who looked even angrier than John. "What the fuck do you want?"

Max peered down at John, and I saw it. That look. It was the same one Max gave me the first time we'd met when I'd interviewed for a sales position at his company. Disgust masked as indifference. Max had treated me so badly that I'd literally stormed after the fleeing prick to tell him a thing or two about why he should never, ever, ever dismiss me. I hadn't known at the time he suffered from a phobia he'd been determined to conquer, but what did that matter? At this very moment, Max was looking at John's thin legs with revulsion.

Something inside me snapped like a tightly

wound piano string. It was one thing for me to be subjected to Max's affliction, but like hell would I ever—*ever!*—let Max hurt my brother.

Okay. Fine. I'm a fifteen on the protective scale.

As I opened my mouth to tell Max he should take a flying fuck out of my life, John leaned forward and punched Max in the dick.

Max doubled over with a loud groan, and John took another swing at his face, sending Max flying back.

"Jesus, John!" What the hell was the matter with the men in my life? They'd all gone completely caveman?

The news crews took no time surrounding Max and snapping pictures or videos.

"You ever hit my sister again, they won't find the body!" John yelled and slammed the door.

Hit me? What in the world? "John! What the *hell* is wrong with you?" I yelled.

"You think I don't know, Lily. I watch TMZ."

He did? Since when?

I rushed to the door to see if Max was all right, but John blocked me.

"Move!" I yelled.

"Hell no." He gripped the top of his wheels tightly. I had zero chance of opening that door without fistfighting my big-ass brother. I could only reason with him.

"John, he didn't hit me."

"Then what happened to your arm, Lily?" His eyes zeroed right in on the black, blue, and purple mark on my elbow.

"I fell."

"Bullshit."

"Come on. Who hits a woman in her elbow?"

John took a moment, likely seeing the light. "Then how did you get that bruise?"

"Max and Patricio were fighting and knocked me over. But no one hit me." Damn those paparazzi and their constant lies.

John shook his head in disgust.

"Hey! If you want to be mad at anyone, be mad at Patricio for cheating on me."

"Patricio? The guy who proposed to you at dinner last week?"

I'd brought Patricio to my parents' house for the first time about a week ago. That was when he'd asked for my hand—a complete shock to everyone. My parents liked him well enough—or perhaps they were a bit starstruck?—but I'd also recognized the slight flicker of disappointment in their eyes. They probably liked Max more. He'd taken care of things—doctors, bills, legal action—after my accident and had been the only person who'd assured them I'd be okay when they were losing their grief-riddled minds. Saying yes to

Patricio would be like closing the door on their hopes that Max and I might reconcile someday. Anyway, it was a little awkward being put on the engagement spot like that, but I'd had to do the right thing and tell him the truth: I would think about it. Patricio, being the actor he was, took it like a gentleman.

I gave John a nod. "Patricio fucked some actre—"

The door buzzed, and my eyes went wide. *Dammit. It's probably Max coming to seek revenge or something really unspectacular.*

"Move!" I instructed John.

John reluctantly rolled out of the way.

I opened the door and stumbled back, nearly falling on my ass as someone pushed inside my apartment. For a split second, I thought it was Max trying to get at John, but it wasn't.

"Patricio?" I gasped his name.

He stormed into my living room with Max on his heels, their bickering drowning out the screaming press crammed into my doorway.

John slammed the door shut, and I took a seat at my small dining room table in the corner, now feeling completely exhausted.

On the opposite end of the spectrum were Max and Patricio, who looked like two uncastrated Rottweilers, spittle flying every which way as they screamed with their noses an inch apart.

"Fuck you! You prick!" Max raged. "I should've done the time and ended you when I had the chance."

"I'd be afraid, but I know choo are a pussy!" Patricio snarled back, his accent always becoming thicker when he got excited. "You don't have the balls for a woman like Lily, and it kills you that I do!"

"That's the problem. You think having two balls means a woman for each. It takes a real man to love one. Only one!"

"Adeline and I are not fucking!" Patricio made fists with his hands. "I told you this ten minutes ago! Those were old photos. We are only co-workers now."

Whoa. I popped up from my chair. "Is that where you went, Max? To see Patricio?"

Max looked at me, flustered as hell. "Yes. I had my assistant track him down."

So Max had ditched me at his hotel room in my moment of need to go and hunt down Patricio, who was likely staying at another hotel down the road. Recently, he'd been staying with me when he came to town, but before we were seriously dating, Patricio had a usual place he liked.

Max continued, "He can't ruin your life like this. Especially now that you're—"

"He's *my* boyfriend, Max," I barked. "He

cheated on *me*, and it's my issue to handle." *Jeez,* he was behaving just like John—Mr. Protective.

Patricio threw his arms in the air. "I did not cheat on Lily. Adeline is my costar."

Is that Patricio's story? If so, why hadn't he told me? And why didn't I buy it?

"Oh really? Let's call Adeline and ask her!" Max roared.

I didn't know what to say. The only thing I knew for certain was that Max had crossed the line when he'd given that look to my brother and then went butting in my relationship. As for Patricio, I wasn't sure if he was a cheating "man-cunt," but he sure as hell kept the news about his costar a secret and that did not evoke trust.

Patricio and Max went at it again, and I deflated back into my chair, propping my good elbow on the little dining table. John and I watched as these two educated, refined men devolved into WWE, trash-talking gorillas.

John flashed a look my way. "You know they're both totally in love with you, right?"

"I think they're in love with themselves," I said.

"Don't know about that," John said, "but I know whipped when I see it. They've got it bad for you."

"Well, too *bad.*" They didn't have what it

took to be *the one.* I stood up. "You're both fired."

Max and Patricio continued their vicious rants, faces pressed together.

"Did you hear me?" I yelled. "Get out! I won't marry either of you."

Max and Patricio shut their mouths and stepped back from each other.

Hands planted at my sides, I gave a nod. "Yep. That's right, guys. I'm done. Like, super done. Don't want anything to do with either of you, so congratulations." Their fight last night, which was clearly being continued right now in my living room, proved that their highest priority was their male egos.

Alpha men should be renamed to "all about me" men.

Panting with rage, Patricio frowned at me. "But what about the baby?"

Huh? "What baby?" I asked.

Patricio, who'd stepped away from Max, pointed at him. "The one *he* just told me about when he came tearing into my hotel room. How come choo told him and not me? Eh, Lily!"

My eyes shifted to Max. "But why would you—"

"Lily, come on." Max stepped toward me. "The morning sickness? The nausea? You can't believe I wouldn't catch on."

Jesus. Well, now I know why Max ran off to

go find Patricio. He thought I was knocked up when really that awesome acid-reflux fun was a symptom of severe stress, something I had been dealing with since the accident. Also, Patricio and I had only had sex a handful of times given we'd only started dating a few months ago and saw each other when he had filming breaks. When we were together, it was always with a condom, and I was on the pill for non-birth control, flow-related reasons. Add all that up, and the chances of my being pregnant were zero point zero, zero, zero.

I opened my mouth to set them straight, but John elbowed me in the thigh. He gave me a quick look, as if to say "Hold up, sis. Don't say a word."

I snapped my mouth shut.

John cleared his throat. "I think it's time for you two to leave. Lily needs her rest."

I resisted scoffing. What the hell was John up to?

Max and Patricio exchanged looks.

"Is this really what you want?" Max asked.

"Yep." I stood and crossed my arms over my chest.

"Fine then. I'm done. If you want to talk, you can find me in Chicago," Max said. He wasn't merely mad at Patricio, he was mad at me, too. Was it because he thought I'd been knocked up by Patricio?

Anger flickered in Patricio's green eyes, but he did his best to smile at me. "I will call you tomorrow."

"Guys, I don't care what you do," John said, "because you both gotta go."

Max and Patricio snarled at each other and then left. The noise of the tabloid a-holes filled my apartment for a moment and then faded out once the door closed.

The second they were gone, the steam evaporated from my body. I walked over to my couch and plopped down, hugging a pink throw pillow to my chest. My head was spinning and my heart felt like it had gone through an obstacle course. *American Ninja*-style obstacle course.

John appeared with a glass of water in one hand. "Here. Take this."

"Thanks." I took the glass.

"Are you really pregnant?" he asked.

"Not a chance."

"That will make this easier, then."

"Easier how?" I asked.

"They're in love with you, Lily. And you're in love with them."

"I'm not."

"Don't dick me around. I know you. Better than anyone, and I see the look in your eyes when they're around."

Okay. I did love them both, but in entirely

different ways. Patricio was like a best friend, and he was handsome and fun. He felt like the man I should want to marry, the safer choice for my heart. I also believed that our love could grow over time and that he would make me happy. My love for Max felt like riding a roller coaster without any restraints or seatbelts. Our passion was intense, consuming, and dangerous. He could suck me in so deeply and quickly, but he could also break me. Regardless...

"I can't love a cheater, and I can't love a man who," I searched for the correct words, "who makes the people I love feel like garbage."

John understood exactly what I meant. "We both know Max's heart doesn't match up with his brain. You can't blame him for that any more than you can blame me for being in a wheelchair."

How could John be so compassionate? And so right? Max's disorder wasn't who he was. It was an involuntary behavior.

He continued, "And Patricio seemed very adamant that he's a victim of that tabloid bullcrap. I think you'd understand something like that."

I sneered at John, who was once again completely right. "So what are you saying?"

"I think you should let them show you what

they're really made of while you figure out which is the right one."

"And?" I asked.

"And let them believe you're pregnant."

"I can't do that." We weren't on some stupid sitcom. I was a grown woman who owned and ran a business that would be in serious trouble if I didn't find a way to pick up sales. "I don't have time for games."

"Lily, let's be honest. Neither of us have had it easy. And given who you are and what you've been through, you deserve a man who will make you happy. I can't think of a better way to flush out their intentions than a baby."

True. Maybe. I didn't know. "That is so, so wrong."

"Is it?" he asked with a sly smile.

"Uhh...yeah. And it could have the opposite effect. Some men marry their pregnant girlfriends out of guilt."

"Or they run for the hills, which is something you'd want to know now. You are planning to have kids, right?"

I shrugged. "Eventually."

"Then the only thing you're doing is preventing a disaster. Let them believe the lie and let them prove to you that they're the right guy. Better to know now before there's an actual baby."

Fuck. This was so deceitful. Then again, Max

always accused me of lacking the backbone to go after what I really wanted, even if it called for some ugly decisions. Also, in the case of Max, part of my reluctance to be with him had to do with the question surrounding what sort of father he might be. Still...

"I can't," I replied. "It's cruel to play around with people's emotions that way. I'm going to tell them tomorrow."

"I think you're making a mistake. Because you can't tell me, without a doubt, that either of these guys really deserves you, Lily." John reached out and grabbed my hand.

"Thank you, John. You're a real turd, but I love you anyway."

"You're a woman-dick, and I love you more."

I laughed. "I know you do, which is why I need you to back off. And to stop punching my ex-boyfriends in their penises."

John wheeled to the door. "Never. Call me later."

I watched him leave. Thankfully the paparazzi had followed Max and Patricio, who had probably kept up their bickering and given them a nice show. All was quiet on my doorstep again. *For now.* But something told me my life was going to get fuglier before it got better. I still had a failing business to deal with and a mess of a love life, the worst part being that I didn't really know where to go from here. A first for me.

Hey. At least I'm not pregnant.

chapter seven

Saturday morning, I awoke in my full-sized bed with a delicious stretch and yawn. A good night's sleep really made a world of difference. So had a big salad and heaping bowl of spaghetti for dinner last night.

"Good morning, honey," said a deep voice.

Huh? I whipped my head to my right and found Max tucked into bed beside me. "What the hell are you doing here?"

"Hey, don't ignore me, *principessa!*" Patricio's deep voice radiated from my left.

"Gah! What the hell?" I scrambled to the foot of the bed and hopped out.

"Lily," said Max in a domineering tone, "get back here this minute. We are going to take turns making love to you so you can tell us who is better."

Patricio nodded. "*Si.* I must know who is the best fuck, Lily. This is the only way to settle things."

Holycrazyexboyfriends! "Get out!"

Max shrugged, looked at Patricio, and they started making out.

"Shit!" I rocketed into a sitting position from my bed, my body covered in sweat. *Dear Lord.* That had been the weirdest dream of my life.

I staggered from bed and stumbled to the kitchen. My body still felt heavy and tired. I needed a few weeks off, not just one night of solid sleep.

I went to my small kitchen—Formica brown counters and cabinets with ten layers of dried, lumpy white paint—got my coffee maker going, and checked my cell. I felt grateful to see nothing from Max or Patricio, but super ungrateful to see a text from Danny, who was my old roommate from Chicago, where I'd lived when I worked for Max. When I came back to California, she moved in with her boyfriend, Calvin, but we still texted all the time, mostly about our boyfriends. She was not a fan of Patricio's, but I always thought it was because she'd been a huge Maxwell Cole fan.

Maybe she was onto something. I stared at the picture attached to her text. It was of Patricio dancing with Adeline at some crowded nightclub, their hips pressed tightly together and his arms wrapped around her midriff.

Danny: *You gotta dump this scumbag, honey.*

"Wow." I pushed my hands through my hair. I had heard what Patricio said last night about the pictures being from his past, but my gut twitched with doubt.

Me: *I hate men.*

The wavy dots on my screen told me her thumbs were tapping away.

Danny: *Have you learned nothing?*

Me (frowning and getting out my power digits): *Like what? That men suck?*

Danny: *You need to make up with Max. There is no other. FYI, he's still in my top five.*

My mouth sprang into the O position. As in "Ohhh…she did not just go there." While we'd been roomies, one of our running jokes—not really a joke—consisted of comparing notes about our "lists." These were the men who occupied our minds when the "power washer" in the shower was set to "stress relief."

Me: *I'm telling Calvin, you horny perv.*

Danny: *Who says C-man isn't in on it? For your reference, I offer role-playing wig—evidence #3.*

A pic of a brown wig, sort of like Max's

hairstyle, popped up on my screen.

"What! Ewww…" I pulled back my phone with utter disgust. "Keep your kinky to yourself, girlfriend."

> **Me:** *TMI. TY. Adios.*
>
> **Danny:** *FU. BTW, when are you coming for a visit?*
>
> **Me:** *Not sure. Have business to run.*
>
> **Danny:** *Jeez. Thanks. You open a new shop ten minutes from my apartment and you won't even come by for a coffee? WTH, L?*

I simply didn't understand, but that knot in my stomach had a horrible premonition. This time, I dialed Danny, who answered immediately.

"What do you mean 'my new shop' is only ten minutes away?" I asked.

"Well, well, well…hi there, stranger! How the hell are ya?"

"Very bad. You have no clue."

"Could that be because I was right about Patricio?" she offered.

I sighed. "Not now. What did you mean about the store?"

"You really don't know?"

"No."

"How's that possible?" she asked.

"What? Tell me!"

"Okay! Sorry! Do you remember my friend who's dating that day trader?"

"You mean that guy Gary, who works out of his parents' basement?"

"Yeah. That's the one. But now he works at M.S.—"

"Morgan Stanley?"

"No. Milford and Schleppy. They run it out of his friend's parents' garage."

Gary was moving up in the world. Literally.

She went on, "Well, my friend said that Gary said that he heard through another friend, who's some big investment broker, that Maxwell Cole took that building he owned downtown and sold it to a private investment firm."

I'd heard about that because my "Maxwell Cole" Google alert remained active—don't judge me—but it had said nothing more than Max sold the building.

"So?" I asked.

"So then a few weeks ago, LLL opened. The store takes up the entire bottom floor."

"And?"

"And I went there yesterday. It's a cosmetics store and there are lilies everywhere—the walls, their logo, and the packaging. I bought some skin lotion and lip gloss. By the way, Lily, the place is amazing. It's like visiting girly heaven."

What? Huh? No. Nuh-uh. Fogettaboutit. Not possible. Olivídalo. Bullshit. Pa-leez. "You're fucking with me."

"No."

Blinking, I held the phone to my ear with my shaking hand.

She continued, "It's beautiful, Lily. The kind of place where you walk in and instantly feel at home, but in a cool way, because my home is a pigsty and stresses me the hell out. But if I had a magic home on a cloud to hide from the world, that would be it."

What. The. Everliving. Hell? "You're telling me that Maxwell Cole secretly opened," deep breath, "a cosmetics store?" Deep breath. "With lilies everywhere?" Another deep breath.

"How's it possible you don't know?"

Max. That's why. That was what he'd been doing these past months. But why keep it from me?

"Danny, let me call you back."

"Sure. Just promise you won't forget. I mean," she chuckled, "it's not every day my best friend's hot ex-boyfriend opens the nicest cosmetics store I've ever seen in tribute to her. Did I tell you it brought tears to my eyes?"

None of this made sense.

"I'll call you right back." I hung up and dialed Max, but it went to voice mail. "Max, you already started this new company? Why would you not tell me?" I drew a breath. "Call me." I hung up and grabbed a mug from my cupboard, my mind a mess of emotions. This was so like Maxwell Cole. He did what he wanted. And why had he not said anything? He'd had every opportunity to mention it.

It all made me wonder, though, if his return to my life wasn't part of some bigger plan, because starting up a new company was big, big news, and I hadn't heard a word, which meant he'd been keeping it a secret from everyone.

Why?

I glanced at the clock on my microwave. *Crap.* I was already running late. I opened the store at nine on Fridays. I scrambled to the bathroom to get myself together, trying not to think about how badly my heart hurt—the pictures of Patricio with that other woman, Max keeping secrets from me. I simply couldn't understand why they behaved like this.

A half hour later, I pulled into the back lot behind my building. My boutique was one of five shops that occupied the quaint little block filled with art galleries, souvenir shops, and small restaurants. Even though people came from all over the world to vacation in Santa

Barbara or go to college, this section still had that small-town charm.

I walked down the narrow driveway, out onto the sidewalk, and to my store. The moment I shoved the key into the lock, my shop neighbor LaSandra called my name. She was a silver-haired woman—not sure from what country—but she made the best fudge and caramel apples in the world. She also sold magazines and newspapers. A very strange combo.

"Good morning, Lily!" she said with an unusually chipper tone. Normally, we'd bump into each other after closing when she looked exhausted and ready to call it a day.

"Hi, LaSandra." I twisted the key and popped open the door.

Wearing a bright yellow summer dress, she walked over, grabbed my free hand and sandwiched it between hers. "Our prayers have been answered."

What is she talking about? "Prayers for...?"

"You haven't heard?"

"Nope." *I'm far too busy getting face time in the* Enquirer.

"There's a new owner who's generously offered to lower our rents by ten percent." She unexpectedly wrapped her arms around me and squeezed. "It's a miracle, Lily. I was considering closing my shop after my lease was up—I just couldn't afford the increase." She released me. "But a decrease? This is wonderful! I can advertise for the holidays and make a profit this year!" She hugged me again and then trotted off to her shop.

Meanwhile, my mind buzzed, trying to understand it all because no one ever lowered rents. Not in California. And the owner happened to buy the place right around the same time Maxwell Cole walked back into my life?

I slid my cell from my pocket to call Max again but paused. Now was not the time to get into it with him when I needed to open the store. Our next conversation would require a solid hour of talking. Okay—screaming.

I flipped on the lights and set my purse behind the counter as the door jingled.

"Ciao, Lily." My head snapped up to find Patricio—wearing black slacks, a red button-down shirt, and a gray fedora—standing in the middle of my front door, holding a coffee.

"Patricio, what are you doing here?" I didn't know how much more of their drama I could handle.

He shrugged his brows and smiled. "Am I not allowed to visit you?"

"Not when I'm trying to get my shop ready and your presence will do nothing but give me the urge to commit murder."

"So you are upset?" Patricio approached me and set the coffee on the counter. It had "Lily" written on it, so I knew it was a white mocha.

Dammit. I love those.

"Lily, listen to me. I was not with that woman. You know not to believe the garbage they print in the tabloids, *si*?"

I narrowed my eyes. What I knew was that Patricio used to be a world-class player and might not have hung up the ol' love gloves like he'd claimed. "The tabloids might lie, but pictures don't."

"It is like I told you, Lily—or was it Max I told?" He shrugged. "No matter. It is like I said; I was with Adeline a few years ago. The pictures are old. We are simply working together now."

I stared at him with one raised brow. "Then why keep it a secret?"

"I did not wish to remind you of Max."

I wasn't buying it. Yes, Adeline was Max's sort of ex—they'd been casual lovers—but Adeline was a movie star. I saw her picture all the time—magazines, on Netflix, and at the checkout stand. Patricio had to know that.

"So," I crossed my arms over my chest, "you want me to believe that you had a fling with Adeline many years ago, but kept it a secret from the world. And then you also decided to keep it a secret that you're doing a movie with her—a movie that I would see eventually when it comes out." I hoped he saw the flaw in his bullshit "secret" excuse.

He stuck out his hands. "Okay, okay. I didn't tell you because I did not want you to see the truth in my eyes and feel jealous."

"What truth?" At this point, I really couldn't wait to hear what garble would be coming out of his mouth next. *This is getting comical.*

"We have done a lot of kissing in the movie, and yes, I am a man and enjoyed it—just a little. But this is very different from what I have with you, Lily." He took my hand and cupped it between his. "I have something with you that I have had with no other woman."

"A death wish?" Because right now, I could see it in his eyes—the man was acting.

Patricio made a little laugh and then raised my hand to his lips, planting a kiss. "Silly Lily. We have true love."

He lowered his head, and I snapped my hand away before he could plant another phony kiss.

"Patricio, I have no idea what's going on, but I'm not buying your bullcrap. And, frankly, I'm not sure how you obtained the best actor in Italy status because you're the worst liar ever." I simply wasn't sure what he was lying about— loving me or cheating on me? Either way, it wasn't good.

Patricio's bright green eyes narrowed on my

face. "And you, Lily, are the weakest woman I have ever met."

"What?" I snapped.

"You let Max poison your opinion of me, didn't you? You listened to his lies and allowed him to turn you against me." Okay, now Patricio wasn't acting. The anger was just as real as the tinge of frustration red on his handsome face. "What did that asshole tell you, eh, Lily? Eh? Did he say I took advantage of his sister? Or that I don't love you? Because before you go believing what other people say, you might want to attempt to give a man the chance to give his side of di story."

Jesus. I felt my shoulders sag with exhaustion. He was right. On the other hand... "Like you gave me the chance to explain why Max was kissing me the other night?"

"That was different. I caught you in the act."

"Okay. Fair enough, Patricio. But tell me this: why didn't you call me when those pictures of you and Adeline came out? Why say nothing?" It made him seem that much guiltier.

"I planned to call you later, but I wanted to make you jealous a little first. It seemed only fair after I found that asshole's lips on your mouth."

"That was pretty low."

Patricio took a deep breath. "Yes. It was, but now I know that your head must be all crazy with the hormones and tings."

By "tings" I assumed he meant "things," specifically baby related.

"Yeah," I said, "about that. I need to tell you, Patricio, that I am—"

"No. I am sorry. I am sorry for playing these games with you when you were—are—feeling very emotional. And I should only be angry with Max, who has wanted revenge on me since I was with his sister."

"So you don't deny you slept with her?" By my calculations, if she'd been sixteen, Patricio had been about eighteen or nineteen.

"Of course not. She was very in love with me, and I liked her very much, but you know how teenagers are. She started talking about marriage and being together forever—nothing frightens away a young man like hearing that sort of thing—it is only natural at that time in one's life when you want to be free."

Well, the way he'd put it, I supposed I might, *might* see his side. Nevertheless, Max still had every reason to be upset. It was the way of the big brother.

He continued, "Max got very upset when I broke things off with his sister and he attacked me in the middle of a cocktail party my parents were throwing. He has issues with anger, that man. Which is another reason I would never trust him with you, Lily. So even if you do not choose me, I suggest you stay away from him. He cannot be trusted."

Okay, that sounded like a red herring. And wasn't Patricio the one who'd attacked Max the other night? That being said…

"Thank you for the advice, Patricio, but I am not getting back together with him."

"Of course not. You are in love with me and are going to have my baby."

"No. I'm not. I'm not having your baby. That was just some—"

"What!" He slammed his fist down on the counter, making the coffee cup jump. "You are going to kill our baby?" he yelled.

Whoa. "First off," I held up a finger, "don't yell at me. And second—"

"You cannot do this, Lily! You cannot take this baby and—"

"Ohmygod! Will you stop and listen? I am *not* pregnant with your baby!"

Patricio's eyes went wide and then wider. His handsome face went from upset to enraged. "You…you…" He shook his finger in my face. "I knew it! I knew you were fucking that Max behind my back." He began ranting in a long string of Italian words I did not understand spare one: *puttana.* "Slut" in Italian.

I crossed my arms over my chest. *Lorrrd, if he'd just shut the hole in that hot head of his for one minute and listen.*

I stood there as Patricio screamed at me, his arms up in the air, waving all around. Strangely, it sort of reminded me of the way he danced.

After several moments, me waiting patiently for him to finish his giant man-tantrum, he said one final thing: "You and I are through! *Finito!*" He turned and headed for the door.

"Wait, but..."

He was gone with a jingle before I could finish, leaving behind only the angry static in the air.

So...Max thought I was pregnant with Patricio's baby and he still wanted me. Patricio thought I was pregnant with Max's baby and then called me a whore and dumped me.

Wow. Just wow. But my brother had been right. The baby variable really had shown me their true colors.

"Well, you're right about one thing, Patricio. We are *finito*," I mumbled to the closed door. I would never let a man speak to me like that in English or any other language. He hadn't even given me the opportunity to explain. Still, I needed to set the record straight. I couldn't have him going after Max or taking some sort of revenge.

I slid out my phone to text Patricio.

Me: *I'm not pregnant, you idiot. But, yes, we are over. Arrivederci!*

I set down my phone and covered my face. *Dammit.* How had things gone so quickly from walking up a hill toward a happier place in life to sliding down back into the muck?

But as I stood there, looking around my empty store, at ten past the hour—not a customer in sight—I felt that churning in my stomach. Discomfort, knotting, nausea. It was like my body wanted to tell me something that my mind didn't want to accept. Could it be the fact that I had been seriously considering marrying Patricio without really getting to know him? Was it that I'd opened this store, knowing my chances of making it a success were nearly impossible? I had ignored the facts because I'd been focused on having something of my own, something to control, perhaps? Or was it the fact that I kept lying to myself, looking for distractions and pretending I was over Max when I really wasn't?

I groaned. "I need my shrink."

chapter eight

"So you're having doubts about your recent choices." Sitting in a brown armchair in front of me, notebook in hand, Clara looked over her black reading glasses at my face. "Tell me more about that."

I looked out the window to our side, which overlooked her English garden and the stone pathway leading to a small dirt lot on the other side. It was the one thing I loved about Clara's home office, the whimsical countryside charm as you approached the separate back entrance of her two-story cottage-style house. It made a person feel like they were somewhere safe and happy. Even her clothes—white cardigan, jeans, and flip-flops—made me feel more relaxed, like I was only talking to a friend. Who charged one hundred bucks an hour.

"It's more than that," I said. "It's like a part of me knows I'm going in the wrong direction, but I don't know what the right direction is."

Even now, as we spoke, I felt all twisty inside. "And the other part of me feels angry as hell because this isn't me. I don't do self-pity. I don't wallow."

"What do you do?" She pushed her dark bangs off her forehead.

"I focus and go after what I want. I fight. I knock down barriers." It was the only way I knew how to live.

"Maybe you need to use that same wonderful drive of yours and focus it inward for once. Use it to figure out what you really want—actually, strike that. Use it to figure out what you *need*. But, Lily, promise me you'll take some time and really think about what your stomach is trying to tell you before throwing yourself into something."

"You mean something like Max?" I asked.

"You can't deny you have very strong emotions for him."

"No, I can't. But I'm not going to risk getting hurt like that again, if that's what you're worried about."

"I merely said you should take time to really think about what you need. You've been through a lot, and it's not unusual for people in your position to distract themselves with work or new relationships instead of addressing the real issue."

"The issue is that Max and I will never work

out. I'm here, and he's there." I held my hands apart as if showing her the size of a big fish I'd caught. "I mean, that man…" I sighed. The way he'd looked at my brother. The way he'd run off and started a "Lily" company. He was so…so…*ugh*. I didn't know. "He's not good for me." But I couldn't deny the attraction and the sexual power he had over my body. It remembered him, craved him, and went full-blown gaga in his presence.

"You two never truly had closure. I recommend talking to him. Tell him calmly what you feel, and then say goodbye if it's really what you want."

Again, she was right. I kept hanging on to Max because we hadn't really ended things. Six months ago, I'd made a mess of his life—and mine—then I asked for his forgiveness and he'd basically said see ya. I needed to really end things with him—a) so he could move on, and b) so I could, too.

"Thanks, Clara. I appreciate you making time for me last minute."

"That's what I'm here for. Let me know how it goes."

It's going to go like shit and you're going to feel like shit, because your head is up your ass. Max is too good for you. And you know that's the issue.

Thank you, asshole voice.

I grabbed my purse from the floor and stood, feeling annoyed with myself for allowing such ugly thoughts to kick me while I was already down.

"At what point will I stop being my own worst enemy?" I asked.

Clara gave me a little smile. "Never. Because you're human. You're also your biggest fan."

"So I'm a narcissistic self-hater?"

"Split personality all the way," she replied with a smile.

"Ha. Not funny."

She dropped her smile. "Who said I was joking?"

"Okay. That's really not funny." I frowned.

"Sorry. Just a little therapist humor." She stood and gave my arm a squeeze. "You're doing fine, Lily. Just try to remember what I said and start using that tenacity on yourself. I'm here if you need me."

Okay, self, get ready to rumble. "Thanks, Clara."

I felt a little lighter as I left her office and traipsed through her garden out to my car, which was really a big old van with a lily pad logo on the side. Not so cool, but I needed it to haul inventory.

As soon as I slid behind the wheel, that annoying heaviness took a seat on my chest.

Okay. Focus. What do I need? What do I need?

I needed closure with the two men in my life. I needed to say goodbye to Patricio, even if I felt angry with him. I also needed to see Max and really explain where my head was at. If I didn't clear out the muck, I wouldn't be able to find room for what I needed: space for me. And if I didn't do that, I would keep hopping from one thing to the next, trying to fill some void in my life without truly knowing what the void was.

I started my engine and headed to my apartment. I would call my mother on the way and ask her to look after the shop while I was gone. Today, I'd completely baled and couldn't afford more lost sales even if miniscule. She loved coming in and helping me from time to time, but she would freak out getting to be in charge of the entire thing herself. She was a model worrywart.

This moment proved to be yet another milestone in my life: accepting help from others, something I'd never quite mastered.

One step, Lily.

I'd left Patricio two messages while on my way to LAX, a two-hour drive but worth the trouble because tickets to Chicago were cheaper compared to the local airport. On the third attempt to call Patricio, I knew he simply didn't want to speak with me, but this was no longer about him. This was about me. *That's right. I'm being selfish for once! Totally selfish! Boohoo for you, men!*

"Patricio, I didn't want to do it like this, but I need to get a few things off my chest. First, I don't want to marry you or see you anymore. Seems silly to say that after you said we were over this morning and you called me a whore—" *I still can't believe he did that. A-hole!* "—but I know you can be a hothead, so I didn't want you thinking this is a fight we'll recover from. It's not because I am cheating on you with Max—I'm not. And that kiss, well, there's no excuse, but it just shows I'm not ready to commit to you or anyone until I settle my past. Speaking of pasts, I don't know if you slept with Adeline again, and maybe I don't really want to know, but I'm not ending things because of her. It's because we're not right together. And I'm sorry things ended like they did because..." My eyes unexpectedly started to tear up. Why? Why was I crying? "Because I really enjoyed," sniffle, sniffle, "our time together."

Patricio had been the first semi-normal relationship I'd ever had. Okay, maybe not semi-normal since he was a celebrity and our relationship occasionally made the tabloids. But we'd gone out on real dates, unlike my relationship with Max, my boss at the time. He'd taken me on his corporate jet to a fashion show in Milan after asking me to be his ugly-aversion therapy tool. We'd ended up connecting in the strangest of love-hate relationships of all time. Then, that night at the party, after the fashion show where I'd danced with Patricio, Max and I got in a huge fight. He'd completely lost his cool seeing me with another man, like I'd lost mine seeing him with Adeline. The result was Max taking me back to my hotel room for an angry, mind-blowing fuck—my very first ever—that opened up a can of worms I hadn't been expecting. I had felt, as maybe I did now, that we didn't make sense and it would only lead to utter heartbreak. That was what I believed, like an idiot, who couldn't accept a good thing when she had it.

I let out a sigh and then cleared my throat, to finish the message. "Patricio, I wish you the best whether it's with Adeline or someone else. Goodbye."

The moment I hit the end call button on my console, I immediately felt lighter. Better. My stomach even relaxed.

I was finally on the right track.

chapter nine

After picking up my rental car at O'Hare, I headed straight to Danny and Calvin's. I would sleep on their couch and have the comfort of knowing that Danny would be there for me after I said what I needed to say. To Max's face. But that would be tomorrow morning.

Tonight, because of the hour—almost eleven o'clock—we were going to have a late dinner at their apartment.

The moment I hit the nearly empty freeway, my phone started chirping like mad. My hand twitched with the urge to pick it up off the passenger seat, but at this very moment, my little silver RAV4 rental was approaching the spot where I'd wrecked my car on the opposite side of the freeway.

I took a breath and moved into the fast lane, the closest I could get to the exact spot. I remembered the location because there was an In-N-Out directly to the side of the road. Funny the things you remember when your life flashes before your eyes.

I stepped on the gas and tightened my hands around the steering wheel. My jaw clenched, and I ground my teeth. "You don't fucking scare me. Fuck you. You don't fucking scare me." I blinked and released a breath, glancing at the marker—invisible to everyday passers—in my rearview mirror. "Ha! That's right. Suck it, accident spot!" I laughed and the sound of sirens filled my ears.

Oh shit. The multicolored lights in my mirrors nearly blinded me. I looked at the speedometer. *Ninety-eight? Oh no.* What had I been thinking? I flipped on my blinker and began moving the car to the right shoulder. I felt like such a dork.

My car now stopped, I reached for my license and lowered my window. "Hello, officer. Would it make a difference if I told you that I almost died right back there seven months ago and got a little carried away, telling my demons to fuck off?"

The man, with his dark short hair and husky build, gave me a frown.

"Okay, now that I just said that aloud, I get how crazy I sound. I mean, who celebrates surviving a car accident by speeding?" I sighed and handed over my license and rental agreement.

He gave it a glance. "Lily Snow." He looked down at me. "Wait. You're the billionaire breaker."

I held back a groan.

He continued, "My wife really loves her gossip magazines."

Golly gumps. How awesome for me. "Everyone's gotta have a vice."

"Your story really shook her up. I've never seen her cry like that."

"Sorry?"

"When that guy gave the press conference—what was his name?"

"You mean Maxwell Cole?"

The officer snapped his fingers. "That's the one. When he gave that press conference and told everyone how much he loved you even after you told all of those lies about him."

I whooshed out a breath. "It was a mistake. A really, really big mistake," I muttered.

The officer handed back my things. "If it makes you feel any better, a lot of people, my wife included, were extremely upset—all of those horrible things the press said about your looks. And then the accident. Man—" He shook his head. "Everyone thought you were dead. Even I couldn't look away from the television when they were pulling you out of the wreckage. I'm surprised someone isn't making a movie about you."

Seriously. That would be the most boring movie ever.

"So what happened?" the officer asked. "Did you and Maxwell Cole ever get back together? The *Inquirer* says you did."

Did this man really expect me to discuss my love life with him—a stranger—on the side of a freeway?

Well, he does have a gun. He was probably used to getting his way.

"It's for my wife," he clarified, likely realizing how nosy he sounded.

"I, uh...I'm sorry to tell you that Mr. Cole and I parted ways."

"Oh. Can I see that license again?"

What the hell? Did he just imply that the speeding ticket would be issued because he didn't like my answer?

Yep. I think he did.

"But...I'm going to see him tomorrow." I shrugged coyly. "So you never know what might happen."

The officer thumped his hand on the top of my car and smiled. "You have a good night and drive safely, Miss Snow." He walked off, muttering, "Can't wait to tell her. Lucky night."

Alrighty. That was some weird shit. And honestly, I'd had no clue there were people out there fanning over my and Max's story. How bizarre.

A movie. Pfft!

I hit the freeway again, and by the time I pulled up to Danny and Calvin's apartment building, it was well past midnight. I found a spot on the quiet street, turned off the engine, and finally looked at my phone.

Three messages were from my mother panicking about the lights in the store. "Honey? Can you remind me where the switch is? I don't remember." She'd been at home cooking dinner for my father when she'd left that gem. "Honey, I haven't heard back from you yet. Are you alright?" The next few messages were funnier than the last, basically my mother admitting that she could handle finding light switches in the morning, but that I shouldn't worry. She had "everything under control."

The next few messages were from my brother begging me to end his misery because my mother had called him twenty times in a panic about running the shop by herself for a few days—"She thinks she's babysitting nukes! Fucking shit, Lily. Kill me now."

Then, finally, at the bottom of the list, I saw a message from him. *Max.* I pressed play, and his voice sounded deep and cold, the heartache palpable.

"Lily, we need to talk." He stopped speaking, but I could hear his soft breath. "Call me," he said, almost whispering, like a man praying for his suffering to end.

Dammit. I have to end this. I started the engine up again and pulled out onto the street. I couldn't let this—his suffering and mine—go on another moment. I would simply need to call Danny along the way and tell her to keep the light on for me. It was going to be a late night.

chapter ten

It took thirty-five minutes to drive to Max's two-story mansion overlooking Lake Michigan. The home, which reminded me a bit of a modern-day castle with its gray brick and stucco exterior, soaring entryway, and high pitched roof, was as impressive in size and presence as it was intimidating. Yeah, just like its owner.

When I pulled up to the wrought-iron gate at almost one in the morning, I wouldn't dare claim I felt prepared. Hell no. The anxiety had worsened. Knots upon knots upon more knots, only made worse by the memories of this place—the long boat dock with twinkling white lights, the big circular driveway with the fountain in the middle, the giant bed upstairs. Every square inch of the property held so many memories of Max and me—mostly good ones of us falling in love—that it had brought me right back. I felt like I was stepping into the past. One I didn't mind being in.

I lowered my window and pushed the intercom button. After a few minutes of no response, I pushed it again.

"Who the fuck is it?" said a groggy gravelly voice.

I almost stopped breathing. Even now, over a stupid intercom, his deep voice did things to me.

I pinched the bridge of my nose. "It's, uh...me. Lily. I'm here to talk."

A moment passed and then another. Finally, the gate buzzed and rolled back.

Crap. My heart went into overdrive. I could do this. I could say goodbye and move on. Couldn't I?

Like the first time I entered Maxwell Cole's home, he did not greet me at the door. I entered the foyer with the vaulted ceiling and large staircase, encountering darkness.

"Max?" I shut the door behind me.

"Up here," his voice boomed.

His bedroom. Not such a great idea.

"Down here," I retorted.

"You came to my house in the middle of the night. You want to talk? I'm up here."

I gripped the staircase railing. *You can do this, Lily. His bedroom is only a place.* Not like it held a special power over me. Still, every piece of my body shook with anticipation. *Fuck. Get a hold of yourself.*

"Fine." I went up the stairs, taking one step at a time. At the top, I turned the corner and stopped in the darkened doorway. "Max?"

"Here." His voice echoed from inside the room that brought back endless provocative and emotional memories. This was the room where he'd once taken me hard, held me soft, and made me feel so loved and beautiful that I had ripped out my own heart and handed the damned thing right over. *Here are the keys to your new heart, Max. Drive it around for as long as you like, just don't dent it. Oh, and while you're at it, can you drive into me again, because your cock is amazing.* Every sensual, elicit memory came crashing down at once as the delicious scent of Max and his cologne infused my brain.

Suddenly, I was right back where we left off. None of the nightmares, the heartache, the mistakes felt real, but somewhere in the back of my mind, that little voice kept telling me over and over again that they were. And if I chose to ignore reality, we would only end up repeating our mistakes.

Be strong, Lily. Just tell him what you came to say.

"May I turn on the lights?" I asked softly.

"Why are you here?"

All right. Play it that way. "I came to get

something off my chest."

My eyes gradually adjusted to the room, and the bit of light coming through the window caught the shape of Max's lean physique. He sat at the foot of his bed, shirtless, wearing only boxers or shorts or something. His arms, which I knew were ripped to perfection, were crossed over his exquisitely chiseled chest. I literally began aching for him, the warmth of his skin and the heat of his mouth on mine.

"Why are you here, Lily?" he repeated sternly.

Clearly, I enjoy torturing myself. "When I saw you last, I said it was over, and it is. But it felt wrong to end things like..." I drew in a quick lungful of air, trying to steady my pulse as the tears began streaming down my face. Telling yourself you were going to say goodbye was not the same as doing it.

"Like *what*, Lily?" he growled.

I couldn't quite come up with the words. "You mean so much more to me than ending things with yelling. And with lies." I exhaled. "So I guess I'm here because I needed you to know how much you've meant to me. Oh, and I'm not pregnant," I muttered. "Patricio and I always used..." I cleared my throat, trying to come up with diplomatic words. "We were very safe. In every way. So it's impossible." *God, I sound like an idiot.* My nervousness was annoying, because I hadn't done anything wrong sleeping with Patricio. *Yet, you clearly feel guilty.*

"So you flew all the way to Chicago so you and I could have a proper goodbye."

"Yes. And I'm not pregnant."

"I got that part."

I wondered if he felt relieved or indifferent or...well, I guess it didn't matter.

"We also need to talk about your purchase of my building and the company—the one you didn't tell me you started."

"All moot points given why you're here, I'd say. All of that can be undone since you wish to say goodbye." The coldness in his tone made me wonder if he was getting ready to put up a fight. Because Maxwell Cole was many things, but he wasn't a quitter. That man didn't let anything get in his way when he wanted something.

"I'm serious, Max. We need to let us go."

The room filled with an uneasy silence.

"All right, then," he finally said, "if it's a proper goodbye you're looking for, strip and lay on the bed."

"Sorry?"

"Take off your clothes and get on the bed," he demanded in a slow deep voice. "That is why you're really here, isn't it, Lily? Because you wanted to feel my cock inside you one final time." He wasn't joking around, and my body knew it. Every inch of me sparked with adrenaline—heart pounding, skin tingling, and my nipples tightening. His rough words had struck a nerve. An erotic one.

"Answer me, Lily," he said, his voice stern.

Had I flown all this way because I needed to be with him one last time? I didn't know, but I couldn't lie. I wanted him. My body craved everything I knew Max could make me feel—love, utter despair, need, ecstasy, and loss... I would lose myself the moment he touched me. And I wanted to.

"Have you been with anyone else?" I knew it was unfair to ask, but I wanted to know.

"What the hell do you think?"

That was a no and possibly his way of pointing out he hadn't given up on us. I had.

In reply to his question, I stripped off my shirt, pants, and undergarments while he watched in silence. It felt oddly arousing to undress for him, but my body had always pleased him. He liked looking at me, and I liked him looking.

My knees unsteady, I walked over and stood in front of him, naked, my chest heaving with anxious breaths.

He gripped my hips with his large hands and pulled me to his mouth, placing a kiss on my stomach.

I gasped quietly. He felt better than I remembered, righter than I remembered.

With one smooth motion, he pulled me down on top of him and rolled me onto my back, diagonally across his king-sized bed. He quickly settled his warm body between my legs, using his muscular thighs to spread my legs wide for him. The weight of him and the warmth of his smooth bare chest pressing against my hard sensitive nipples sparked little contractions deep inside my core. I ached to feel him enter me and release that tension.

He tipped his body to the side, slid his shorts down past his firm ass, and freed his cock before grabbing my hands and sliding them over my head. The length of his hard shaft pressed into the wet and ready valley between my legs, but he held back what I really wanted.

He kissed me forcefully, but his lips were warm and sweet and could possibly be the last thing I'd ever want touching mine. He kissed the sides of my mouth, my chin, my forehead, and nose. I felt a drop of wetness trickle down the side of my cheek, and it took a moment to realize it wasn't my nervous sweat or emotional tears. It was him.

In a million years, I couldn't imagine that a man's tears could touch me or make me love him so deeply—they were always seen as a sign of weakness. But this man. This man. So strong and confident, not giving a shit about showing how he felt, it stripped me down to nothing. Bare. Vulnerable. Cherished.

I poured myself into our kiss and ground my hips against his erection, letting his length slide between my slick folds. He let out a soft groan and rocked himself into me, increasing the friction over my pulsing c-spot.

Oh, God. I felt like I was going to come already. Nobody could turn me on like Maxwell Cole because no man knew me better than him.

Panting hard, I threaded my fingers with his and raised my hips again. I needed him so badly, I wanted to scream.

He released one hand and slid it between our bodies, grabbing his cock and placing the head at my entrance. He made teasing little circles, mixing my wetness with his.

"Please. Please," I panted, unable to stand it.

Instead of ending the torture, he positioned the head of his shaft just so, allowing me to feel him there, but not giving me more.

He deepened his kiss and once again pinned my hands above my head. I felt so lost in him, in my need for him, and he knew it. He wanted to show me what I was trying to say goodbye to. He wanted to show me that he, too, had power in this relationship and that his might be stronger.

"Please," I gasped.

"Is this what you want?" He flexed his hips, pushing only a centimeter into me before pulling out again.

"Yes." I panted.

"You really think you can walk away from me, from us." Torturously, he pushed the tip inside again, making me lose my mind. "Say it, Lily. Say goodbye now." This time, he went an inch deeper, enough to give me a taste of the fullness and pressure only his dick could deliver.

"No. I can't. Please just—"

"That's right, Lily. You can't, because you know how good I feel inside you." He thrust hard with one fluid motion, drawing a sharp gasp from my mouth.

Every inch of my body lit up and pulsed with sensual tension.

My fingers flexed into his palm while he pulled out and thrust into me again, pushing all the way.

"Fuck, Lily. I missed you." He pumped again, and I threw my head to the side. How was it possible that the sheer act of his hard shaft being inside my body made me feel like this? Like I could reach every star in the sky. Like I wasn't me anymore, but merely a body he owned. A body he commanded and knew how to torment so deliciously.

I slid my hands from his and moved them to the sides of his face, never wanting to stop or let go of this moment.

Max pumped harder, and I rocked my hips against him, wishing somehow he could get deeper. Not possible. He already touched everything that made me who I was.

Max lifted his torso and pillared his arms to the sides of my head while pistoning his thick cock into me. "Look at me, Lily."

I opened my lids and saw his hooded hazel eyes locked on my face.

"Don't ever leave me again," he said.

I didn't know how to respond. I'd come here to say goodbye—for me. For my sanity. But feeling him move inside me, his body pressing me into the mattress, his cock sliding in and out, only made me think of staying. Forever.

I came hard, and he came harder, jetting his cum deep inside me in time to each delicious contraction of my muscles. He pushed deeper, willing himself into me. Me inviting him.

I felt it then. That strange buzz that seeps into your soul when someone takes a piece of it. Or maybe connects with you on such a level that your cells shift position to welcome them. I didn't know, but something changed inside my head. I could not deny how much my soul craved him.

Breathing heavily, still inside me, Max rested his scruffy jaw on my collarbone. He said nothing, but there wasn't anything to say. The moment was perfect. His heat, his smell, the taste of his salty tears on my lips.

The moment was perfect.

And I felt terrified all over again. Terrified.

The question was, could I really stay? And if I did, would I fuck it up again? Or would he?

chapter eleven

Max and I slept for a few hours, and he made love to me again, this time flipping me over onto my hands and knees, taking me from behind while his thick fingers made sure I came harder than before. The third time that night, I'd been sound asleep in his arms, spooned by his tall lean frame, when I felt his velvety head slowly nudging its way into my tender entrance. He'd ridden me hard tonight, but this time he took me so slow and gentle, I'd thought I'd died and gone to hell—sinful, sinful, sinful. No doubt about it. Because the way he worked his hot shaft in and out of my entrance made me want to sign over my soul and never look back. When he came that third time, he stayed inside me and passed out. I couldn't come. Not again. But feeling his body wrapped around me, inside me, his delicious scent permeating my lungs, couldn't have felt any more like heaven than heaven itself.

The next morning, Sunday, I woke to an empty bed, cool gray sheets, and drowned-out daylight filtering through the khaki curtains.

Holding the sheet to my chest, I sat up. "Max?"

I listened closely. He might be in the kitchen, making coffee. Or in his office, making calls.

I slid from the bed, threw on one of Max's large dress shirts he had draped over an armchair in the corner, and traipsed down the stairs. His den—an immaculate space with stacks and stacks of magazines in the corner— was empty. I made my way to the large, open kitchen with giant windows overlooking the lake. I immediately spotted a note on the granite counter.

Lily,

I wanted to let you sleep. You looked exceptionally tired this morning, though I cannot think why. When you're ready, meet me at LLL so we can further discuss this goodbye of yours. Properly.

Callahan is waiting outside to take you.

Love,
Max, Your Boss

I smiled. "My boss, huh?" I muttered. All

right, I'd give him "boss in bed." And I couldn't deny he'd played me well last night, because I found myself questioning the decision to end things. Were we really as broken as I'd thought? It was difficult to imagine after he'd reminded me of how well we worked together. *Perfection.* We were perfection last night.

So what if I *chose* to let go of all my fears and simply *chose* to be happy with Max? I wanted to. I did. But I couldn't see how to get there. Not without learning how to permanently discard my unwelcome self-esteem gremlin. *Don't feed it after dark!* I would have to let go of it and a lifetime of viewing myself as spoiled goods—flat out sexually undesirable. But the negativity almost felt embedded in my DNA, like a billion years ago, nature decided that some of us had to be ugly. Otherwise, how would the beautiful women shine? People required something to compare to, right? What was smart without stupid? What was strong without weak? What were giant knockers without sporty boobs?

All right. Enough. I had to put a stake in the ground. At some point, I needed to accept responsibility for how I felt. It was like Clara said; I needed to apply my tenacity to something new: me. Easier said than done? Probably, but what did I have to lose other than a lifetime of this self-deprecating bullshit.

As for Max, my tiny revelation didn't mean that my fears about him weren't valid. Max's affliction was a variable completely outside of my control and it was up to him to conquer it.

But, God, how I wanted to help him do it. *See. You love him. You love him that much.*

Still, I felt stuck. My heart wanted this so badly, but my brain kept pushing me back. *It won't work. It won't work.*

S*hut up, you little fucker.* The sane me took the reins. *I'm going for it.* If last night showed me anything, it was that Max knew me better than I knew myself. He knew how to ground me and help me see a future together.

Hell, the guy cried for you!

When I was in his arms, it wasn't a fucking ugly life, it was fucking beautiful.

❧ ❦

At ten past ten, I arrived to LLL, entered, and stood there in awe. *Holy shit.* Max had taken the old lobby of Cole Cosmetics and turned it into something ripped straight from my dreams.

This wasn't a cosmetics store—walls plastered with photos of beautiful size zero women with flawless skin and perfect cheekbones—this place looked like a vacation on the planet of pampered real women. *How the hell did he do this? To a fucking lobby? In downtown Chicago?*

I literally had the urge to remove my little white blouse and taupe pencil skirt and just run naked.

Relaxing spa-like music played in the background while a gentle stream of water trickled from a crack in a wall made of large river rocks. It flowed into a tiny stream that snaked through the room only crossable by tiny wooden bridges or raised stepping-stones. Throughout the space, product stood on large wooden pedestals with shelves carved inside them to hold more products. Couches, Zen-looking coffee and tea bar, hand-carved coffee tables, and a neck massage station made this look more like a getaway in a meadow of peacefulness.

Wow. It was magical. I looked around at the happy women perusing, sampling lotions, and smelling perfumes in small clay bottles. A group of older women sat on moss green stools in the corner and faced a young brunette, who appeared to be showing them how to make homemade avocado masks.

It was really, really cool. Relaxing, serene, beautiful. Like a fairytale rather than a store.

The best part was that there were no photos of "perfect" women that screamed "you're not good enough."

Taking my time to let it all soak in, I strolled through the store, inspecting the products. There were no anti-aging cream this-or-thats (because what the hell was wrong or ugly about aging?). There were no complexion-refining foundations either. Instead they were called skin-nourishing foundations "to make your skin as happy as your heart." Even the dang mascara had a squishy-positive name called flirty lashes for a "flirty mood." Everything was positive and geared toward being good to yourself or having fun. Not one single message of "you've got a defect and we'll help you fix it."

"This is just a pilot store to test out our concepts, but do you like it?" Max appeared at my side, wearing his usual expensive faded jeans that made any woman within eyeshot salivate. He also wore a white button-down shirt, rolled up at the sleeves, exposing just enough skin and muscle to trigger instant ovulation.

"Like it?" I replied. "Are you insane? I love it. But...what does the LLL stand for?"

"Lily's Lovely Lies." He smiled. "Because if it weren't for you, I never would have done this."

"Oh." So it was his way of saying that everything happened for a reason. Specifically, I had believed some very big lies about him— that he had only used me to debunk the claims that woman made in her book about his disorder.

"Of course, that's our little secret, between you and me," Max added. "The marketing campaign has been focused on women telling their husbands that they're going shopping, but really they're sneaking off here. To be pampered. We'll be testing out some other stylistic and marketing concepts over the next few months before launching five new sites."

"Max, it's incredible." I couldn't stop my eyes from darting around and drinking in the subtle details—the white lilies painted on the sage green walls, the flow of the floor plan, the soft lighting, and even the natural packaging of the products. He'd turned shopping into more than simply buying products but a secret indulgence. I grabbed a bottle of Heaven Made Your Hands hand cream and flipped it over. *Whoa.* I leaned toward Max and whispered, "Eighty bucks?"

"Premium product."

A little disapproval shimmered in my eyes. That was steep.

"We give ten percent of profits to charities who support women," he added.

"That's better."

"Can I show you the rest?" he asked.

Frankly, I'd seen enough. He'd taken my dreams and made it reality. It was simply unbelievable and part of me even felt jealous. I mean, it would've taken me a decade to put something like this together on my own. Max had waved his billionaire wand and created a pilot store in less than six months.

However, despite my awe, he and I needed to talk. I'd decided on the way over that what I needed to hear from him was how he really planned for all of this—us—to work out. Yes, I was looking for excuses to say yes instead of no.

"Can we go somewhere private to talk?" I asked.

"Right this way." He dipped his head and gestured toward a set of stainless steel elevator doors toward the back. That was when it hit me again. This entire store used to be the lobby of Cole Cosmetics. My eyes did another sweep. *Truly amazing.*

"And your mother is completely out, right?" I asked as we made our way to the elevator bank.

Max's expression went from proud and smug to positively glowing. "I never have to see her again."

I could hear the sense of freedom in his voice. His nightmare was finally over.

"I'm so happy for you, Max. Really."

"Thank you." He scanned a card on a security pad and the elevator doors slid open. We stepped inside.

"Just like old times." Max hit the button for the top floor and flashed a mischievous little grin.

We'd once made out in this elevator, and I'd never forget. His lips and hip action had almost made me come in five seconds flat.

I turned to him, wanting to say something, but forgot. He looked so tall and handsome in his jeans and linen shirt, but his messy hair and unshaved jaw really made the goosebumps flourish.

"Yes?" he said.

Keep focused. Must have serious conversation. No sex. No sex. No sex.

"Uhhh...so I hear you sold this building."

"Not exactly. I transferred the title to LLL."

This was a huge building in the middle of downtown Chicago with views and premium office space.

"The entire thing?" I asked.

"Lily, I was dead serious when I said I wanted us to start this company."

"But you went ahead and started all this without ever consulting me."

He cleared his throat and scratched his scruffy jaw. "Yeah. Well, this was supposed to be a wedding present. A surprise." His tone was sharp.

"Oh." I honestly didn't know what to say. I could see how if he'd thought I'd say yes to his marriage proposal the other day, that this might be the next logical step for us. Still, it was a bit presumptive. Okay, really presumptive. And also touching.

The doors chimed, and we exited on the top floor. Like the storefront downstairs, the space had been overhauled and turned into an oasis with sage green walls and khaki burlap-upholstered furniture. Potted palms and a small water sculpture in the lobby area by the elevator gave it the appearance of a waiting room for a world-class spa. The floors, once polished cement, were now done in small river rocks to make it feel like you were outside in a meditation garden. *Jesus, who wouldn't want to come and work here every day? "Boohoo, I have to go to the office and feel peaceful."* Today was Sunday, so the office staff wasn't working, but I could genuinely imagine the place filled with smiling, peppy employees. *Me included.* This was so not the Maxwell Cole I'd met eight months ago—that man had been cutting edge, high-concept fashion, with sharp edges and an even sharper tongue. His office of stainless steel and minimal decorations had been a reflection of his icy disposition.

"What do you think?" he asked.

"What do you think I think?" I pointed to my smiling face.

"I wanted you to feel at home here, and I

know how much you love being outdoors."

If he'd done all this as a wedding gift, I couldn't imagine what he might do if I had a baby or got his name tattooed on my ass. *Or maybe our baby's name tattooed on my ass?*— something big and permanent.

"It's really nice, Max."

He lifted a dark brow. "Nice, huh?"

I grinned. "I said really."

He chuckled with a tinge of cockiness. "All right, Lily. Let me show you something else that's 'nice.'"

We walked past a reception desk that held a few personal effects—coffee mug, framed photo I couldn't see, and a name plate that was really an etched rock. I immediately recognized the name.

"You hired Keri back?" I asked.

Max nodded. "She's been asking about you."

Keri was a gorgeous tall redhead with an eye for fashion and a hot boyfriend who lived in New York and worked for a top dress designer, Babs Levine. When I died, I wanted to be buried in one of Bab's hand-stitched sequin dresses, like the one Max had bought for me in Milan during our first weekend together. It was the same dress he'd torn off my body right before taking my virginity and fucking me against a wall. I'd never, ever be one of those women who wished for a do-over on the virginity-loss thing, unless you were talking about doing it over with Max. *Goddamned stud.*

My core began to ache and tingle with the thought, my skin sparking with hypersensitivity and increased blood flow.

I made a little cough. "Uh...tell Keri I said hi and that I'm still waiting for her to dump her man so I can snatch him up."

Max glared with intense hazel eyes.

"I want him for the free clothes," I said facetiously. Keri always had the nicest couture, compliments of her man, who received tons of freebies at work.

"Why the hell would you need free clothes?" Max asked judgmentally.

"Because I'm a girl?" Poor or rich, we all liked free.

"Anything worth having is worth paying for." He stopped in the doorway of his office and gestured for me to enter.

I behaved casually, but my insides felt like the guts of a clock—wheels turning and cranking and spinning.

I walked three feet inside and stopped, covering my mouth. "What is this?"

Max ran his large hand through his messy hair. "This is supposed to be your new office. The desk reminded me of the furniture you used to have in your bedroom."

Ohmygod. Once the sterile, masculine-looking office of the infamous Maxwell Cole, this newly decorated corner space overlooking downtown Chicago had light pink walls with etchings of white lilies. There was an overstuffed white couch with lily-shaped pillows and several armchairs, all surrounding a natural wood coffee table. Even the desk—a whitewashed antique-looking thing—was totally laid back and outrageous wonderful.

It was all so...incredibly thoughtful. I wanted to cry.

He continued, "But given you told me last evening you came to Chicago to say goodbye—"

"Max, let me explain—"

"No. Let me. As you pointed out, I was foolish to assume you would be waiting around six months after I gave no indication whatsoever of a reconciliation. But it took me thirty-three years to find you, Lily, and it never occurred to me that you'd fall in love with someone else. So now I see that I've made two errors since we met: one, not telling you how much I loved you before the scandal, and then taking six months to tell you where my head was at. So please don't see all this as some sort of scheme meant to pressure you to come back. I simply never doubted we'd have a future together and, true to my flawed nature, I wanted everything to be perfect—for you, for us. This was all meant to be a new life and fresh start for us."

My eyes teared. He had seen this company—and the store and this office—through the lens of a man who was already married. And now that he'd explained that, it made sense. Maxwell Cole was obsessed with perfection— he couldn't help it. So why wouldn't he take the same obsessive approach with us? His six-month absence from my life probably seemed like a necessary sacrifice to him in order to make everything just right.

I took his hand. "Max, you beautiful eccentric man, I can't begin to articulate how blown away I feel right now. I mean, I get what you were doing, and as long as I live, no one will ever measure up to you." I looked around the room. "This is all so..." I blew out a breath. "It's wow."

"But?" He crossed his arms over his chest.

"But I'm confused about us. My heart wants you so badly; my body wants you, too. But my head keeps telling me bad things, and I don't know how to get past it."

"So you really are saying goodbye."

I didn't want that. I really, really didn't. But I didn't want to jump into this and fuck it all up again and get hurt or hurt him. I also needed to get my act together. It was time to shake some old habits and learn to love myself. As for him...

"This is what I wanted to talk about, Max. I feel like we both have a road ahead of us before we can be together. You have some things to work out, too."

He shook his head. "That's the point you continue to miss, Lily. We are much stronger together. We challenge each other. We definitely don't take each other's shit."

All true.

He walked over to the desk and pulled out the comfy-looking exec chair. "Take a seat, Lily. Because this is where you belong. Here, with me, living your dream."

I stood there, next to the coffee table only a few feet from the door, frozen in conflict. Meanwhile, Maxwell Cole looked like his usual, confident self, able to convince anyone of anything. A natural born salesman. And who could resist that face? Or body. Or hell, that long dick of his.

"I think I should..." I closed my eyes, barely able to resist the pull. But I had to do what was right here. "I should go."

"Lily," he growled.

"I need a little time. That's all."

"I think you need something else altogether." He walked toward me, unbuttoning his pants.

My eyes shifted side to side. "Uh...what are you doing?"

He walked past me, shut the door, and faced me. "Turn around." He pulled out his hard cock and my eyes stuck to it. My body immediately reacted with heated throbs between my legs and tingles erupting on my c-spot. My nipples tightened into little pebbles and my mouth went dry. *God, I so want him.*

"I said turn around," he demanded in that low authoritative voice he always used when something displeased him.

I didn't reply because my mind was a crazy hot mess. *I should go before he fucks all sense of rational thought from my mind.*

No. Stay. Look at that thick hard dick. You know you want it.

Max stepped up to me, grabbed my hand, and placed it on his hard shaft. He dipped his head and pushed his lips to mine, pressing his other hand to the back of my head, deepening the kiss. The other hand he used to guide my fingers around his girth. Not that I needed help. I knew exactly what I wanted to do with him. I began to stroke him firmly, enjoying the feel of the soft velvety skin sliding over warm steel. I imagined him inside me, pumping hard, hitting that sweet spot that made me come in earth-shattering contractions that radiated through every nerve in my body. I loved how Max took control in the bedroom, how he knew how to use his body and deliver hours of mind-blowing fucking. The man made sex into an art form where he skillfully balanced giving and taking. He took and he took hard, but what he gave in return was sinful ecstasy.

Still, sometimes a girl wanted to take control, and if there was one sexual memory of the two of us that repeatedly seeped into my fantasies, it was my first encounter with Max's magnificent cock. My first encounter with any man, for that matter.

Stroking him firmly, I broke away from our kiss and looked up at him. A smile curled my lips as I lowered myself to my knees.

Max's gaze was hard with lust, but the moment I ran my tongue over his tip, he threw his head back and let out a deep, throaty groan.

I'd only done this once before—to him, obviously—but I still recalled the salt of him on my tongue. And now, like before, feeling him between my lips, sliding in and out, made me excruciatingly wet. I loved having power over his body like this, knowing that the deeper I took his cock in my mouth, the hotter it made him.

I ran my tongue down the underside of his shaft and up again to the tip, cupping his balls and squeezing gently.

Max flexed his hips and groaned again. "Fuck, Lily. That mouth of yours is fucking amazing."

I smiled and sucked him back between my lips, wrapping one hand down at his base since there was no way in hell that big dick would ever fit all the way inside my mouth.

I began moving faster as Max pumped his hips, thrusting himself in time to my movements. He placed his hands at the back of my head and threaded his strong fingers into my hair. His pace quickened, and I knew he was close. Honestly, so was I. One little flick of my c-spot, and I would be jumping off the O-cliff with a huge splash.

"Fuck, Lily," Max panted his words, "I'm going to come."

I continued, feeling insanely aroused by the sound of his voice and the dirty thoughts of letting him come somewhere other than inside my mouth. Maybe on my tits or on my face—something I never would've considered in the past.

Max pulled away. "Stand up and turn around."

He quickly helped me to my feet and bent me over the back of the armchair. He lifted my skirt, pulled down my panties, and thrust into me from behind. My breath whooshed from my lungs as he hit the spot like a bull's-eye with the tip of his cock, triggering an orgasm that started deep inside. I froze, unable to breathe or think or speak. Max withdrew almost completely and then slammed into me again, triggering another delicious contraction.

"Oh, God. You're so fucking tight, Lily." He withdrew and repeated the thrust, this time reaching around to stroke my c-spot. That was it for me.

I whimpered with another hard orgasm that washed through my body, my nails digging into the chair.

"Yeah, that's right. Come for me, Lily," he whispered and pressed his fingers in time with his pistoning cock to draw out every last contraction.

I thought I might lose my fucking mind.

Just as I began to float down from cloud nine, Max straightened his spine, grabbed my hips, and fucked me harder. His hips slammed against my ass, and he drove into me again and again, so deep it almost hurt.

"Fucking hell, Lily..." he said with a gravelly voice and leaned in. His dick twitched as he poured his cum inside me.

After several long moments, he made a few tiny jabs, releasing those last drops, before he exhaled loudly. "Goddammit, Lily. You know I can't let you go."

At this moment, I didn't want him to. "Yes, boss." I smiled.

He slapped my ass hard. "That's Mr. Cole to you."

❧ ❧

I could hardly see straight while Max and I put ourselves back together, but as I hiked my skirt down, I suddenly realized we had fucked in broad daylight and one entire side of the office was made of windows. One tall building down the street had a view inside.

"Please tell me those windows have that reflective stuff on them," I said, feeling mortified.

Max laughed. "Of course. I'm not sharing you with anyone ever again. Not even visually." He gave my ass another smack. "Now get dressed. We need to talk."

"Ouch!" I stood up straight and shot him a look, rubbing out the sting.

He winked. "There's more where that came from if you don't change your mind and tell me this goodbye bullshit is behind—"

His phone rang in his pocket. He slid it out and glanced at the screen. "My apologies. I need to take this." His expression melted from freshly fucked and playful to ice-cold serious. I didn't like it one bit.

"Sure," I said.

He put the phone to his ear, left the room, and shut the door behind him.

Nervous, I quickly straightened out my skirt and walked over to the window, looking for any sign of peeping Toms.

"Lily." Max's deep voice filled the room, and his solemn tone immediately put me on edge.

Crap. "What's wrong?"

He lifted his beautiful dark brows. "Do you remember my sister?"

I'd never met her, nor did I remember her name. The only thing I recalled was that she'd disowned her family at some point, including Max, simply to extract their crazy mother from her life. Max had stuck it out with his mom mainly because she owned the majority share of Cole Cosmetics. As for his father, I got the impression that the man never stepped up for his children, perhaps a victim himself of his wife's sadistic personality.

"The last you mentioned, you were looking for her," I replied. At least, I thought that was right. He'd only brought her up once or twice and not in great detail.

"Yes. And that was the private detective I hired six months ago. He just found her."

Then why didn't Max look happy? "That's great news. I'm so happy for you. But...?"

"She was so difficult to track down because she got married—took another last name—and moved to Argentina."

I suddenly realized how disconnected I'd truly been from Max's life these past months. While I'd been living in my world, trying to get my life back on track, he'd been doing the same.

Idiot. You started a boutique and got a shitty apartment. Max had been trying to lay the foundation of a new life for the two of us and reconcile with his estranged sister. *Shut up, fugly voice. You're a stupid loser.*

"That's good, right? You found her," I said.

"She's sick."

Oh no. "What kind of sick?"

"She's pregnant and something's wrong— the detective is having a hard time finding out details. He's not family, and I've given him strict instructions not to make himself known."

"What are you going to do?"

"I have to leave."

My body recoiled with the thought, but I couldn't be selfish. Not now. "Sure. I understand. If you need anything—"

"Funny you should mention that because I need you to run the ship while I'm gone."

What? "Max, I can't do that—"

"Lily," Max grabbed my shoulders, "the reason you didn't hear about LLL is because I kept my involvement a secret. I worked through my staff and lawyers. But that was only so I could get the initial phase in place and surprise you. I came to see you when I did because it was time to let the cat out of the bag and begin courting retailers. Those meetings will begin tomorrow morning and so will the media campaign about our new venture—you at the helm and me driving the marketing. It's going to be big."

Oh crap. Mr. Perfect strikes again. He'd had this all planned out. Surprising me, making a huge to-do about the company's launch, he and I starting our life together.

He went on, "I have the head of purchasing from the world's most exclusive retail chain and her entire team coming to see the pilot store."

"But I can't—"

"Yes. You can, Lily," he said without doubt or room for negotiation. "I've got the presentation all set. You simply need to smile, shake hands, and talk about our marketing strategy. It's all stuff you've done before." Yes. My background was in sales and, of course, I'd worked for Cole Cosmetics for a brief period as a senior sales manager, so the question wasn't if I could sell or engage with customers. It was that up until a day ago, I hadn't known this company existed.

"Don't you have a head of sales or someone to step in?" I asked.

"You. You were supposed to be head of sales. And no, there is no one else, Lily. We have a skeleton crew in place to support the initial phase, but that's it."

"So…when you say that's it, how many

people are we talkin'?"

"Ten."

"Ten?" My jaw dropped.

"Lily, we're in proof-of-concept mode right now. And frankly, I held back doing any major hiring until you were on board."

Ohmygod. He was just so damned...so damned...perfect. *Dammit! Why does he have to be so domineering and aggressive and thoughtful?* It just killed me to say no to him.

"Lily, I need you to step in for just a few days. I'm sure you can handle it, and considering it took a month to pull this meeting together, I can't risk postponing. This isn't Cole Cosmetics. We're the new kids."

Meaning, when he snapped his fingers, the entire industry didn't jump. Not yet.

He continued, "Everything is in the presentation. Keri will help you with any questions, as will the team."

I sighed. "Max, I really ca—"

"Thank you."

"Max!" I dropped my shoulders. "I have a store to run in California. I can't ditch it."

"Who's running it now?"

"My mother, and she's absolutely terrified of being in charge."

Max slipped his phone from his pocket, dialed a number, and held it to his ear. "Hello? Gladys?"

He's calling my mother?

He smiled and made a little chuckle. "Nice to hear your voice, too."

Whoa. Since when were these two all chummy?

He went on, "Great. I'm great. Even better now that I'm looking at your beautiful daughter."

I narrowed my eyes, but at the same time couldn't help letting a tiny smile sneak past my lips. Max was always so full of surprises and such a shameless charmer.

He listened for a moment. "I know what you mean. She really does look lovelier than ever."

"Hey! That's enough," I protested. "Tell my mom to stop talking about me."

Max gave me his back and strolled over to the window. Yes, I took notice of his broad shoulders and the taper of his muscles that gave his body that perfectly masculine Y-shape.

"Yes, I heard that," he said to my mom. "And I'm very pleased you enjoyed your day at Lily's store." He glanced over his shoulder and flashed a smirk my way. "Especially because I have a very big favor to ask." He listened.

Oh no… Mom, don't you dare!

"Thank you, Gladys," he said, "because a family emergency has come up, and I need Lily here in Chicago for a few days." A long pause.

"Well, I will let her tell you all about it, but I just wanted to be absolutely certain that you're all right with holding down the Lily Pad while I'm away." Pause. "Great. You are truly the best mother anyone could ever ask for." Pause. "I miss you, too."

"What the fu…?" my voice faded as Max ended the call, slipped his cell into his jeans, and cocked his brows. "What the hell was that, Max?" I scowled.

He shrugged. "What?"

"'I *miss* you'?" I repeated his words like an accusation.

Max looked down at his feet and gave his scruffy chin a scratch, making those little bristly sounds. I loved that sound. It was uniquely masculine and sorta turned me on.

"Your mother and I—well, and your father, too—have remained in touch these past six months."

I blinked while his words sank in. Once they did, I was not happy. "You mean to tell me that my parents have been helping you keep tabs on me?"

Max gave me a hard look. "You truly believe they would do that?"

I crossed my arms. "You tell me." They'd kept their relationship with him a secret, after all.

"We only spoke a few times. I think they

were checking on me—you know your mother is an excessive worrier."

"Hey! Don't bad-mouth my mother." It was true, however. My mother's and father's constant worrying had once prompted me to blaze my trail a little further from home. It wasn't that I didn't love them, but space was good.

Now, after everything that happened, I didn't mind their worrying so much, and I sometimes wondered if Max's mother had something to do with that. I'd only met Mommy Dearest the one time, but it was enough to help me understand why Max was who he was and be grateful for my own mom. To Max's credit, he wasn't nearly as messed up as he should be. His mother was as cruel as she was bonkers. She'd even had us stalked by a photographer, who took pictures of Max and I having sex at night in front of his beach house in Hawaii. Long story short, she thought if the world knew he'd been dating a very, very ugly woman, it would deflate the rumors that he had a disorder and save his company. Her company. Maybe it would've worked, but her actions had only helped me believe he'd been using me.

God, if I ever see that woman again, I'm going to punch her down there. Right in the clit. Or maybe I'd break her nose so it would be crooked forever and drive her mad.

"I'm not bad-mouthing Gladys," Max said, bringing me out of a very wonderful daydream of me straddling his mother and beating the crap out of her face. "I think her worrying is sweet. I would've given anything for a mother and father like you have. They're good people and they care."

"Oh, fuck you!"

Max's head jerked back in shock.

"That's right!" I said. "Stop being so perfect and saying all the right things. It's annoying and making me feel all squishy."

Max stepped forward. "You mean you love me?"

I huffed. "That's not the issue."

He pinched my chin. "Then what's the problem, Lily?"

Ugh! He already knew the answer. "Can we *not* go into this right now?"

He tweaked my nose. "Whatever you say, Lily Pad." He stepped around me and opened the door.

"Where are you going?" I asked.

"To the airport."

"Max, no."

"Your mother just told me she had the best day of her life running your store and 'talking with so many interesting people.' I need someone to fill my shoes here, and I can't think of anyone more qualified than you."

I gnashed my teeth together.

"It's my sister, Lily. I have to go. So don't force me to pull the guilt card," he added.

Dammit! He just did! I knew how worried he had to be about his sister, and being the perfectionist that he was, he probably wanted to go to Argentina to be by her side as much as he did to oversee that everything possible was being done for her. Perfectly.

Dammit, he's so awesome. I wanted to kick him and his perfect everything.

"No guilt card required," I said. "I'll stay. If it was my brother, I'd be freaking the hell out."

Max stepped forward, threaded his fingers through the back of my hair, and beamed down at me with those beautiful hazel eyes. "I love you, Lily." He kissed me and this time his lips were soft and tender, exactly like I might expect and want at this very moment when he was pushing me outside of my comfort zone.

"Stop it." I pulled back. "Stop being so damned perfect all the time. It's irritating."

Max winked, pecked my lips, and turned for the door. "Callahan will take you to my house. The keys to your Porsche are hanging on the wall in the kitchen pantry."

"What..." Before I could protest or ask what Porsche, Max was halfway to the elevator on the other side of the floor. Still, I couldn't help trying to assert myself and take back a little control. "I have a rental car! And I'm staying at Danny's!" I yelled.

Not expecting a response, I heard Max yell back, "Sure. Enjoy her lumpy cum-stained couch! Be my guest!"

Ewww... Surely her couch wasn't cum-stained. My mind quickly went to work. Danny and Calvin were serious hump-hounds. Anywhere, anytime, and in bulk quantity. They were like the Costco of sex.

My stomach lurched as I imagined laying my body on their sofa, a place where they'd surely fucked a few times each day.

Gross. "Fine! You win!"

chapter twelve

Three weeks went by after Max left me at the helm of Lily's Lovely Lies, and I did, indeed, take the helm. From day one, I found myself stepping into a role I was born to do. The overjoyed buyers and executives rolled in on a daily basis, wanting a piece of the LLL pie once we launched. "It's what our customers have been waiting for." "LLL is the next big thing in our industry." "We want exclusive rights to your next season of products." What I realized was that while Max had disassociated himself from the public face of the company, he'd made it clear to the fashion community that he would be very active behind the scenes. So while Max might have initially lost face with some of his customers when the shit hit the Cole Cosmetics fan, he had not lost his reputation as the King Midas of makeup when it came to building winning marketing strategies. Everyone on the business side still saw him as a boy wonder.

As for me, the three weeks apart had helped me to appreciate what he'd meant when he'd said I would be the face of the company. He'd meant it literally. I carried my own sort of "brand" with consumers, mainly as the ugly woman who'd captured the heart of the most sought after bachelor on the planet. To the outside world, my name and face symbolized something I'd not seen before: that beauty is in the heart of its owner.

So corny. I got that. But for the first time in my life, I was really beginning to love being me. Not so much because of external factors, but because I got to see myself through the eyes of others. It sounded strange, I knew. But sitting down with buyers, investors, and media, they all wanted to hear my story and how I'd been inspired to change an industry. If they were women, they told me how much it meant to see someone like me reach for their dream. If they were men, they had daughters, a wife, a sister or mother who told him about how my story meant something to them. The irony was that people seemed to relate to me more when my face was harder to look at, but they still wanted to know if surgery changed my life. Of course, the answer was "not really." I was still me and the change I was after would only come with a lot of hard work.

"But that's why this company's mission is so important," I said in meeting after meeting, discussing LLL's product lineup for next year. "In five, six, ten years, we'll have had the opportunity to influence a new generation of girls. The goal is to get their mothers, grandmothers, aunts or older sisters addicted to our products and our message."

"But the other companies can outspend you, and they're not going to change a strategy that's worked for centuries." Meaning, they'd built their businesses on making women feel lesser.

"Every journey starts with one step," I'd say. "And if we do well and we can show that our business model is successful, others will follow."

"Then you'll lose your competitive advantage if everyone tries to copy your marketing strategy."

"A world full of companies selling self-love rather than self-hate to half of the world's population? Sign me the hell up."

So the more I talked to potential customers—buyers for major retails stores, Internet retailers, specialty boutiques, and hotel chains with high-end spas—the more I realized that I had not been the only person on the planet feeling imperfect and tired of it.

And Max had been right. This was my

dream. This was the reason I'd suffered all those years with a face that made people cringe. It was why I'd been given a big beautiful brain and the drive of a pit bull. And it was why I'd met Max.

Did this realization signify easy sailing? Or that things between him and me were settled romantically? I didn't know. But I knew our relationship was so much more than romance or sexual attraction. And now, after having time to breathe and think, I knew that what we could accomplish together was fucking amazing.

And I loved him for that. I loved him for not giving up.

Just past midnight, as I sat back in Max's king-sized bed, typing away on my laptop, my cell phone buzzed on the nightstand. I looked, and it was Patricio.

Strange. He'd not called, emailed, texted— nothing—since I'd left him that voice message weeks ago. It still stung to think about how easily he'd left me behind, but it had proved I'd made the right choice.

My hand hesitated before finally tapping the glass to accept the call. "Hello?"

"Lily, I must talk to you." His voice was frantic and scratchy, like he'd been crying.

"Patricio, what happened?"

"I must talk with you—in person."

"Why haven't you called me?" And why so desperate to see me out of the blue like this? Did he not understand that I had cared about him? It was not the same crazy chaotically passionate relationship I had with Max, but I'd genuinely felt something for this guy. Then he'd called me a slut, walked out of my store, and never said another word.

I did call him and leave a message to tell him we were over-over.

"This is why I must see you. I need to explain what has happened, Lily."

I sighed and wiped my left hand over my face. I supposed, after everything, I owed him that much. "I'm in Chicago right now."

"Chicago?"

"It's a long story, but I'm helping Max with his...with our...with a business project. His sister is ill."

Max called every few days with updates. It had not been going well. His sister had refused to see him for the first week and her husband spoke no English, so Max's attempts to reason with him did no good.

Of course, Max, being a resourceful guy, got a translator and found out what he could about the situation from the doctors. Apparently, his sister had preeclampsia and kidney failure. They were trying to keep her stable long enough so the baby could be delivered prematurely and survive. Max then started looking into doctors and treatments and finally convinced the husband to talk to Max's sister on Max's behalf. That had only been a few days ago, and Max sounded like hell. "I can't leave, Lily. She's either going to die or that baby will." I'd had no choice but to stay on and assure him I was taking care of things. So here I was, three weeks later. Luckily, Max was very organized with his business, so it hadn't been difficult for me to step in—reviewing data for site locations for the first five stores he planned to open, discussing consumer feedback and tweaking the product lineup, meeting with the contract manufacturer to review volume projections. And then there was the hiring. The headhunter had people swarming her with applications from some of the best and biggest cosmetics companies in the world.

"I see," said Patricio. "You are back with Maxwell, then?"

"No. I mean…" I whooshed out a breath. "It's not like that." I had issues to work out in my own life, which was what I was doing.

"I had wanted to speak in person, but fine. I will put all of di cards on di table," Patricio said with that accent of his, a bit thicker than usual. He was definitely upset.

"Okay?"

"My mother and father are here in town. So

are my sister, brother and their spouses along with my nephews and nieces."

"Uh. Good for you?"

"Lily, they are all here to see you. And me, too, but mostly you."

"Why me?"

"Because I haven't told them that we are not getting married."

Uh-oh. I saw where this was heading. "Then you're going to have to tell them." I had big issues to deal with right now, and his family drama didn't concern me.

"Lily, my mother is seventy-five years old and has a bad heart."

Then why the hell was she flying halfway around the world? "So you're asking me to...?"

"Pretend to be my fiancée—just for a night. Two tops."

"I'm not going to lie to your family, Patricio." What a stupid idea.

"It will break her heart to have come all the way here to meet you only to find out that I've been lying to her—she wants nothing more in this world than to see me married before she dies. That and to go to Disneyland."

Ugh. I rubbed my face. I didn't want anything to happen to his mother, but I couldn't drop everything, fly to L.A., pretend to be engaged to him, and explain to Max why I was doing this favor for his arch nemesis.

"I can't, Patricio. I really can't. And I don't think it's fair asking me this when you haven't even called."

"What was there to say? You cheated on me. And you're pregnant with his child."

"Whoa. I left you a message. I'm not pregnant."

"I lost my phone weeks ago and had to get a new one. But this does not change that you cheated on me."

"I did not cheat on you."

"You did not sleep with Max?"

Errr... "Well, not at that point."

"Lily! So you are sleeping with him now?"

Oh crap. Why were we having this conversation? "You and I are not together anymore, and the only thing you need to know is that I didn't screw around on you."

If anyone had been unfaithful, it was Patricio.

He let out a long sigh. "I miss you, Lily. I really miss you. And I am sorry for the way I yelled at you when we were together last, but you must understand that you broke my heart. So now I ask you for this favor, Lily. I don't want to risk making my mother upset."

Crap. I felt my heartstrings tugging toward giving in.

"You are one of the few people I've ever met who I trust, Lily," he added.

He didn't trust me that much—he'd thought I'd cheated on him with Max.

"Please, Lily. I am begging you. If you ever cared about me, you will do this one last thing."

Dammit. What was with men and the guilt card? "I'll think about it, but sooner or later, you'll have to tell her the truth."

"When the time is right, I will. But she came all the way from Italy with the whole family to surprise me, and I've never seen her do anything like this. She's so excited to meet you. And Mickey Mouse, of course."

God, I really didn't know what to do. On one hand, it felt kind of crappy that he hadn't called so we could end things like they deserved. On the other hand, he'd never received my messages and I did still care about him as a friend.

"I can do brunch on Sunday, but that's it." I could fly in tomorrow night, Friday, after work, spend Saturday in Santa Barbara to check on the store and my mom, and then drive back to L.A. for brunch and head to the airport afterwards. I could definitely use a quick stop at my apartment for some clothes somewhere in all that. I'd borrowed a few outfits from Danny—we'd had dinner a couple times at her place since I'd arrived—and the rest of the clothes I'd worn were quick outfits I'd purchased during my lunch hour at a few boutiques down the block from work. I would've taken a trip over to the outlet stores or Miracle Mile for better work clothes, but as it was, my personal budget was tight. No, I was not making a salary at LLL because Max and I hadn't had time to formally talk about all that.

"Brunch is perfect. Thank you, Lily. I thank you."

My stomach turned into a mess of knots, and I suddenly felt like throwing up. Strange. Now that I'd thought about it, I'd been feeling great up until now.

Patricio's back and so is your acid reflux. A definite sign.

"I'll text you Sunday so you know what time I'll be there," I said.

"Good night, Lily. Rest well."

"Same to you, Patricio."

I ended the call and immediately tried to get Max. I didn't want him surprised in any way or to get the wrong impression. It went straight to voice mail.

"Hey, Max. It's Lily. I know it's crazy early there in Buenos Aires, but I was hoping I'd catch you. I have to go home this weekend—nothing major, but I need to help..." I hesitated, wondering how I could frame the situation with Patricio in a way that wouldn't stir up dust. I really didn't need him worrying. He had enough on his mind with his sister's health. "Well, it's nothing important. I just need to do a favor for a friend and take care of a few things back at the store. Call me later when you can."

The moment I hung up, I found myself staring at the phone. That was the right thing to do. *Wasn't it?* I'd tell Max everything later. At the right time.

Still, why did I feel like I'd made a huge mistake?

The next morning, I scraped my body from Max's cold, but extremely comfortable mattress. My days started at four a.m., so I could answer emails, take care of business expenses, and handle inventory orders for Lily's Pad. My mother, ironically, was kicking ass. I didn't know her secret, but she'd been able to increase sales by fifty percent. A damned miracle.

I then reviewed Max's daily task list—the usual micro-manager bullcrap I used to get when he was my boss, but now included the sort of messages that made me blush. "I jerked off last night, thinking of your tits, Lily." Or my favorite, "I woke up hard, dreaming of your smile." And "I fucking love you, Lily. I can't get enough."

I found his daily emails to be like these

really messed-up love letters I cherished with equal parts of affection and irritation. Seriously? How did he always know what to say to me?

This morning, however, there'd been nothing. Not a peep, not a text or a call.

I hope nothing's wrong. If there was, I'd know, right?

After running forty minutes and getting myself together for work, putting on my basic white blouse and black skirt outfit, I rode in the town car to LLL, with Callahan at the wheel so I could work on my laptop. *Dammit.* This was insane trying to run two businesses.

I groaned, hoping Max would make it back soon—with happy news of course.

"Everything all right, Miss Snow?" asked Callahan from the driver's seat.

"Yeah. I just have way more work than I can handle. Thank you for the ride, by the way."

"I don't mind—it's what I'm paid for; although, I'd imagined you'd be wanting to try out your new car."

Yeah, I'd seen the white Porsche Panamera in the garage with the giant white bow on top, and it was gorgeous. But I couldn't accept frivolous gifts like that—one that had been intended as a wedding gift.

"Even if I appreciate the gesture," I muttered, "I can't let Max spend his money on me." We weren't getting married. We were...well, I didn't know. We were complicated. "We're...friends."

Yeah, friends who just fucked like crazed rabbits three weeks ago. Then I'd given him a blow job in my office, followed by him bending me over the armchair.

I crossed my legs and wiggled my toes inside my black heels, feeling my body sparking with erotic tingles between my legs. The back of my neck felt hot, too.

I pulled my hair up into a sloppy bun and sighed with frustration.

Callahan flashed a glance through the rearview mirror and smiled like he didn't buy what I was selling. I couldn't blame him.

When the car pulled up to the storefront at seven thirty a.m., I immediately noticed a middle-aged, shrill-faced bitch in spiked white heels and a white pantsuit, standing in front of the doors. Perfectly smoothed-out brown hair combed back into a bun, large white sunglasses, and fake red nails as long as my legs told me that this woman was obsessed with image.

Fuck. That's Max's mom.

My immediate reaction was what you might expect: tell Callahan to keep driving. But that little fire deep inside my chest sparked to life. This woman, the antithesis of Max, was a cancer on the soul of humanity. She represented everything I detested in this world—true ugliness. And while I understood that some might ask what separated her from her son, I knew the answer clearly. She didn't care who she hurt with her ideals or expectations. She didn't acknowledge her illness. Max did. She would spit on someone who didn't wear the right shoes for the time of year. Max would cringe, but then pull himself back to Planet Reality and feel a little bad about his behavior.

In any case, after everything she'd put me through—sabotaging my relationship with Max, invading my privacy, calling me a piece of trash—I had a few things to get off my chest.

I slid from the town car, and her hazel eyes—same as Max's but without any sign of humanity—locked on my face, darting from scar to scar. Forehead, cheek, nose. The normal human wouldn't bat an eyelash since I wore makeup today, but she caught every imperfection.

"Well, if it isn't Lily Snow," she sneered.

I walked toward her, resisting the urge to belt her silicon lips and overly Botoxed brow. "Mrs. Cole, what a pleasure. Did Oz run out of flying monkeys to boss around or little dogs to torment?"

Her eyes sort of narrowed, but with so

much plastic surgery, she could barely move her facial muscles.

"Shut up, you ugly cunt. Where is my son?"

"Ugly cunt?" I had a nail file in my purse. Those were great for puncturing jugulars, right?

Don't kill ugly bitch. Don't kill ugly bitch. Don't kill ugly...

I placed my hand on my hip. "He's trying to save your daughter and her unborn baby from dying. Why aren't you doing the same, Maxine?"

The corners of her lips curled down. "What the hell are you talking about?"

She didn't know? No. Why would she? Her daughter had disowned her.

"Your daughter has preeclampsia. She's been hanging on for weeks, trying to save the baby." I'd read up on the condition, of course, learning that if Max's sister could make it to the twenty-sixth week, the baby had an eighty to ninety percent chance of surviving. Anything past that had extremely high chances. Mabel, Max's sister, was at week twenty-two.

Maxine lifted her hand to her overly inflated, artificially puffed-up lips. Tears filled her hazel eyes.

For one tiny second, I felt vindicated—I wanted to see her suffer. But then my heart kicked in, because I sensed she hated herself as much as I did. Nevertheless, this was not my doing, and she did not deserve my sympathy. Not after everything she'd done to me, which only paled in comparison to what she'd done to her children.

"Where is she?" Mabel whispered.

I didn't think it was my place to say. And given the circumstances, I wasn't about to tell the woman to call Max.

"I'm sorry, but I can't help you." I stepped around her and gave a nod to the security officer who stood on the other side of the glass door, allowing employees to enter the building prior to the store's opening.

"Listen here, you disgusting little gold-digging slut," she growled. "I know all about you and your sleazy Italian boyfriend."

I turned and looked at her, wondering what she was talking about.

She went on, "You think Max won't find out what you're up to? You think you can marry into our family?" She stepped closer, putting us two feet apart. The overdose of Coco Chanel nearly made me gag. "I'll never allow it, you fucking little whore."

Involuntarily, I felt my hand ball into a fist and my arm reach out and swing. I landed a punch right on the woman's nose and felt it crack. She screamed and blood poured from her nostrils as she fell back onto the cement.

I felt torn between the urge to spit on her

and the urge to help her up because this wasn't me. I didn't go around hitting people even if they deserved it.

Callahan must've been watching, because he appeared right away. "Go inside," he commanded.

My feet wouldn't move.

The security guard rushed outside, and several employees, arriving for the day, stopped to see the commotion.

All the while, Mrs. Cole lay on the sidewalk, groaning.

"Get some paper towels," Callahan ordered the security guard, who disappeared inside.

From the corner of my eye I saw a young woman, a salesclerk I think, calling 9-1-1. Out of nowhere, two paparazzi began taking photos.

I looked down at Mrs. Cole, and our gazes met for a moment. A flicker of joy sparked in her eyes.

Fuck. She'd done this on purpose. What had I done?

chapter thirteen

Shortly after eight o'clock in the morning, the police arrived to arrest me. Not a surprise. Mrs. Cole had baited me, plain and simple. And what was her endgame?

Wasn't sure.

Maybe she'd hoped I'd go to jail forever or that she'd scare me off from Max. Maybe she wanted to get even for Cole Cosmetics' demise. Either way, I'd broken her nose, and now I was in some sort of trouble, but her behavior only made me want to marry Max to spite her.

No. Stop, Lily. Don't give her any power. I could never allow his mother to influence my actions again or interfere with my feelings for her son. That said, I began to see how easily she poisoned the people around her.

Monster! I thought as I sat handcuffed to a bench, waiting to get booked. Oh, the press was going to have a field day with this.

"Mrs. Snow?" I looked up at a tall, older

gentleman with thinning gray hair.

"Yes?"

"I'm Robert Krane—Mr. Cole's attorney."

Crap. Max knew. Not that I'd thought he wouldn't find out.

"Is he angry?" I didn't think Max would be upset because I'd punched his mother, but that I'd allowed her to get under my skin and had gotten myself into a mess when he needed to be focused on his sister.

"Mr. Cole is unreachable, but your assistant Keri called me. I'm on retainer for LLL and their employees."

"I'm not an employee."

"Yes. Of course, you're the owner—that is what I meant."

I stared blankly at him. "I'm sorry. Can you repeat that?"

He gave me a strange look. "Are you referring to the part about you being owner of the company?"

"I don't own LLL," I pointed out.

"I filed the paperwork myself. You're fifty percent shareholder."

"That's not possible. I never signed anything."

His brows shrugged with confusion, but then he put on his poker face. "I suggest you take that up with Mr. Cole."

Ohmygod. "You wouldn't happen to know if

I also own part of a small shopping plaza in Santa Barbara, California?"

With the same no-tell expression, he said, "Once again, I suggest you take that up with Mr. Cole."

Dammit. So he'd gone off, made me an equal partner and never said a word.

"Sadly, no one knows where he is." Which worried the hell out of me. The last time he'd gone missing, his company had been falling apart. Our relationship soon followed.

"I'm sure he'll turn up soon," said Mr. Krane. "In the meantime, let's work on getting you out of here."

It took about six hours for Mr. Krane to get me out on bail. I still couldn't believe this was happening.

"Aggravated assault?" I'd asked. "But I only hit her once."

"She's currently in the hospital with a broken nose and a cut on the back of her head."

Oops. I guessed she fell. Too bad there hadn't been a cliff behind her. Evil cow.

"I'll be in touch soon with your court dates," said Mr. Krane. "And the judge gave you permission to leave the state, but don't go on any trips outside of the US, and expect to be back here in a few weeks."

"Thank you for helping me," I said and

marched out of the station, feeling thoroughly deflated.

Gah. What a mess. As soon as I hit the sidewalk, several paparazzi greeted me, and I had no choice but to let them have their fill. Nowhere to hide. *Bastards.*

Callahan appeared, and true to his usual nature, he didn't show any emotion. "Sorry I'm late—couldn't find a spot."

"It's okay," I said, ignoring the two men following us for a half a block. I felt so violently ill, I thought I might fall over right there on the sidewalk. "Please tell me you've heard from Max."

"No. But are you all right?" Callahan grabbed my arm to steady me as I began tipping over.

"I think I need to lie down." I'd call Patricio in a bit and tell him I couldn't make the brunch on Sunday. He'd have to come up with an excuse, but hopping on a plane to pretend to be his fiancée sounded like the world's worst idea. I felt sicker than a dog.

"Can we stop by a pharmacy on the way?" Some antacid sounded really wonderful right about now.

"Of course." We walked around the corner to the black town car parked down an alley. Callahan opened the rear passenger door. "And may I say, Miss Snow, that you have a very impressive right hook." He flashed a quick grin.

I bobbed my head. "Thanks, Callahan." She did have it coming.

On the way to Max's, I called Keri to check in on things. She'd already moved all of the meetings into the middle of next week. Thank God today was Friday. Next on my list was Patricio, but he beat me to the punch and called first. The moment I answered, all I heard were screams on the other end. "You should not be with that man! His family is like poison, Lily! Poison! I am going to kill him!" His accent was out of control and so was he.

"Patricio, just calm down."

"Calm down-a? Calm down-a? I tell you about calming down-a! I see your video on the Tweeter! I see you being arrested because of that man's snake of a mother. They are no good for you, Lily!"

Oh boy. I couldn't do this right now. "Patricio, I can take care of myself. I only called to let you know that I can't make it Sunday. Please tell your mother I'm sorry, okay?"

He began yelling some more, so I simply had to end the call. *What a hothead.*

I then texted my brother, telling him I'd been in an altercation and that I needed him to run interference with my parents. If I called them now, I'd have to listen to my mother crying and my father going into a fit.

Me: *tell them I'll call later, but I'm OK*

John: *they're already shopping for tickets to Chicago*

Me: *what?*

John: *the arrest & pic of you hitting that bitch was all over social media*

Oh no...

Me: *please call them and talk them out of it*

John: *What's in for me?*

Me: *UR such an asshole*

John: *what's new?*

I knew he was joking, sorta, but he had to know I was in a shit heap of trouble.

Me: *this isn't a game, John. I need you to keep them out of my hair. And I need mom at the store*

Several long moments passed.

John: *okay. I'll take care of it. Hope you're alright*

"Miss Snow?" Callahan called out from the front seat. "Would you like me to go inside for you?"

I looked up from my phone, seeing that we'd parked in front of a pharmacy. "No, thanks. I'm okay." I slipped out and went inside, seeking out the digestive-assistance aisle. I planned to get one of everything. As I passed by the feminine products, I didn't think much about it, but then a bad, bad thought slammed right into my brain.

Wait. I stopped in the middle of the aisle.

I hadn't purchased anything of a feminine-product nature since my arrival to Chicago. With a shaky hand, I scrounged through my purse and found my packet of birth control pills. I was halfway through the week—that one with the little brown pills meant to keep you on track while you had your period.

No. No...not possible. I felt sick because of stress, right? Same as it had been for almost seven months. I'd also been working harder than ever and that did not help matters. Besides, Max and I were...we were... I wanted to tell myself we'd been careful, like I'd been with Patricio, but no. No condoms. Because Max hadn't been with anyone, and I'd been very cautious. So Max and I had relied on my pills. Same as before.

I hadn't forgotten to take any, had I?

I slid the packet of birth control pills from my purse again. Wednesday. I was on Wednesday's pill. Today was Friday.

Crap. I felt my blood pressure hit the floor. I'd missed two days, and if those two days were when I'd been with Max—

Ugh. Stupid, Lily! Stupid, Lily! In my own defense, I'd been taking the pill for years to help with cramping and the usual sorts of unpleasant stuff, so taking my morning dose was something I did on autopilot. I just did it.

And you forgot.

My heart pounding, I turned slowly. Right in front of my face was the display of little white sticks in fancy boxes. My trembling hand stretched out, and I felt like I was reaching for a nightmare. A big fat nightmare hiding inside an innocuous little box.

I grabbed a three-pack and headed for the register.

The ten-minute drive back to Max's felt like two seconds. Somewhere in the back of my mind, I'd heard my cell vibrating over and over again. Callahan spoke to me, too, but I couldn't hear a damned word. The entire world had disappeared around me, leaving only myself and my frantic heart. I sprinted inside Max's house, through the front door and into the guest bath right off the foyer. I fumbled with the plastic-foil wrapper, tossed the cap on the ground, and did my thing. As I sat there, panting, feeling like I was going to lose my mind, a funny feeling sank in. Why was I panicking? I wasn't all together ready, but I wasn't fifteen. And Max would be happy, wouldn't he? My fear that he'd be a horrible father and mentally wreck our children for not being perfect was idiotic. I saw that now. He wasn't anything like that woman I'd hit today. He was good. He knew who he was. I had to trust him because if anyone didn't have their ugly under control it was me, not him.

I glanced at the stick and felt my innards dissolve.

Plus sign. "Oh shit."

I didn't know how long I stayed in the bathroom, peeing on the other two sticks, wondering how the hell I'd forgotten to take my pills, but the results did not change.

I threw everything into the trash and washed my face with warm water to clean off the sweat. Hanging my head over the sink, I looked into the mirror at my face. What if I had a little girl, and she turned out to look like me? The thought broke my heart. Not because I wouldn't love her, but because I knew how cruel the world could be. I didn't want to watch my or any child endure that sort of pain. I just didn't.

I suddenly felt a huge amount of respect for

my own parents. They'd never once led me to believe they'd had these same thoughts and feelings, but they must've.

I shook my head and patted my face dry.

A loud knock on the bathroom door startled me. "Lily!"

"Max?" *Holy Jesus.* I jerked open the door, and there he stood looking wrinkled and beaten down. "What are you doing here?" I threw my arms around him and hugged him hard.

He peeled me off. "Why weren't you answering your phone just now?"

I blinked up at him, taking in that sublimely beautiful face with several weeks' worth of thick stubble. "You should talk! I haven't heard from you for two days!"

"I forgot my phone at the hotel in Buenos Aires, and I didn't have time to replace it since I had to get to the airport to catch a plane home—the Wi-Fi was also out on the plane. But forget that. What's this I heard about you hitting my mother and getting arrested?"

I winced. "She had it coming."

He shook his head, and I saw the raw anger in his eyes. I hadn't expected him to be so upset.

"I need a drink." Max headed for the living room, where he had a bar in the corner. I followed him, feeling every nerve ending spark with adrenaline.

He served himself two fingers of scotch. "Care for one?"

I stood opposite him across the narrow counter. "No. Thank you."

He took his glass, raised it to me, and threw it back. Frankly, I'd never seen Max looking so volatile.

"Are you all right?" I asked. Because there was a lot I needed to talk to him about—the ownership of the company, our very complicated relationship, Patricio's little issue, but really, there was only one topic I needed to get off my chest ASAP. *Baby.*

He set his glass down and refilled it. "No," he barked in reply to my question.

I was about to ask what happened with his sister when the front gate buzzed.

My lips twisted sideways. "I'll get that."

Max was too busy pouring another drink down his throat, determined to anesthetize himself from something awful.

I walked over to one of the intercoms stationed in the little hallway just off the foyer. "Yes?"

"Lily! You open this gate right now!"

"Patricio? What are you doing here?" *Oh, hell. He must've been calling me from the airport earlier.*

"I am here to see that bastard! Open the

gate."

Hell no. He'd clearly come for a fight, and Max's foul mood would guarantee he got one.

I heard the gate buzz open.

What in the... I hadn't touched anything.

"The man wants to see me? Let him the fuck in." Max stood behind me with a remote of some sort in his hand and then walked back to the living room.

"Are you out of your mind?"

I heard a car's engine roar up the driveway, tires screeching, followed by the front door bursting open. "Where is that disgusting *mudder* fucker!" Patricio pushed past me and stormed into the foyer. "Get your ass out here, Maxwell Cole, you dirty bastard!"

"Patricio!" I grabbed for his arm. "You need to leave..."

"Max! I'm going to beat your ass!" Patricio yelled.

"Go, Patricio. Go!" I tried yanking him out by the arm, but he wasn't budging.

Max appeared in the doorway, rolling up his sleeves. "What the fuck do you want, you piece of shit meatball?"

Patricio pointed at him. "I want to kill you. That's what! You think you can frighten me?"

"Clearly, I cannot." Max went to work on the next sleeve.

Oh shit. They're gonna fight again.

"No. You cannot!" Patricio shook his finger at Max. "And Lily is mine."

"No. I'm not," I protested. "Now go!"

Patricio swiveled on his heel in my direction. "You and I both know that Sunday wasn't really about doing me a favor."

"What favor?" Max looked at me.

"Okay. This is getting out of hand." I looked at Patricio. "I have no clue what you're talking about. You said your mother would practically die if I didn't show up for brunch."

"Because she has wanted nothing more than to welcome you into our family. You don't know them, but they love you already. And so do I! You only need to see it with your own eyes."

Lightbulb. Sunday's brunch was Patricio's underhanded way of trying to win me back.

"So you what?" I waved my hand through the air. "You thought after our breakup three weeks ago that I'd meet your family and just swoon and agree to marry you?"

"Yes. Because I can offer you a real life with a real family. Not some broken twisted devil for a mother-in-law and a lying sister."

Oh crap. Now was not the time to be talking trash about Max's sister.

Before I could say a word, Max charged Patricio and knocked him to the ground. This time, it wasn't funny or sexy or entertaining. It was fucking scary because I'd never seen Max so enraged.

He pulled back his fist and landed a punch right on Patricio's neck.

Oh fuck. I lunged forward and grabbed Max's hand as he cocked his fist. "Stop! You're going to kill him!"

Diverted by my tugging, Max's fist landed on Patricio's shoulder while Patricio gasped for air.

"Max! Stop it!"

"You fucking wanna talk about my sister, you motherfucker?" Max landed another punch right on Patricio's jaw. "You fucking used her! She was fucked up and you only made it worse."

I could see the fear in Patricio's eyes and white-hot rage in Max's. I didn't know what to do.

"Stop! I'm pregnant!" I belted out.

Max's fist halted in midair, but he didn't look at me. Panting, he glared down at Patricio, hate radiating from Max's every pore.

"Max, did you hear me? I'm pregnant. And yes, it's yours. So please get the hell off of him before you make more problems." God knew we didn't both need to end up in jail and with arrest records. I mean, what a complete bummer that would be for our kid. *Don't mommy and daddy look so nice in orange, sweetie? We can't wait to hug you when you're five once we're free!*

Panting, Max remained frozen over Patricio.

"Please," I whispered with a controlled calm, "get off of him."

Max slowly rose, and Patricio rolled to his stomach, still gasping.

I didn't know exactly what I expected next, but Max turned away from me.

"Where are you going?" I asked, watching him head up the stairs. "Max, say something. I'm fucking pregnant."

Without looking at me, he stopped mid-step. "That is very unfortunate." He disappeared upstairs.

I felt my heart drop through a giant gaping hole in my chest and stomach and smash to the floor. I didn't know what to say or do or...

Patricio, hacking for his life and grabbing at his neck, caught my attention.

I let out a breath and then kneeled down. "Are you okay? Can you breathe?"

He nodded. "I told you, Lily. The Coles are poison," he whispered with a hoarse voice.

I bobbed my head. "Maybe you're right."

"Are you really pregnant?" he asked.

"Yes," I whispered. "And please don't call me a *puttana* this time, or I will stomp on your nuts."

chapter fourteen

By the time we pulled up to the ER, about twenty minutes from Max's house, Patricio was breathing again and insisted he would be fine. "I cannot afford the bad press right now."

I was in no mood to argue with the man, and the grief in Patricio's eyes guilted me into taking the same flight home with him versus the first flight out in the morning. Patricio still had family in town, back in L.A., and plans in the morning, so he couldn't wait.

As for me, I needed to be home with people who cared about me. I was pregnant, and as I sat next to Patricio on the plane home, all I could think about was what a mistake I'd made with Max. Or maybe I hadn't? Seeing Max nearly kill Patricio—probably similar to the first time when they were younger—and then walk away from me like that had shown me a side of him that was uglier than anything I'd ever seen before. Maybe I needed this to happen in order to close the doors on us—on him—once and forever, though that was not what I wanted.

Yeah, but you can't pretend that that didn't just happen. And Christ! I was going to have his baby. We'd be linked for life, one way or another.

"You will be okay, Lily." From the seat next to me, Patricio patted my hand. He looked like hell and had bruises on his neck and face, but his green eyes were happy.

"Are you gloating?" I seethed.

He shrugged.

Eeesh. Men.

"I am not happy to see your heart broken, Lily, but I am happy that you now see the truth. Maxwell Cole is not a good man."

Funny, Max had said the same thing about Patricio.

"Well, maybe he's not, but that doesn't change anything." My heart hurt so much that it took everything I had not to cry. My mind kept replaying the image of Max walking away from me. "How can a man say he loves you and then just...turn his back like that?"

"I thought you met his mother?" Patricio said.

I waited for him to elaborate.

"She taught him to be exactly like her," he said. "And he is. You can't change him."

I never believed I could. I had believed that

he could.

I rubbed my face and tried to let it all go. I mean, Jesus. I was pregnant. And my life was a goddamned mess. I'd have to return to Chicago and go through a trial. A criminal trial.

When we landed, Patricio and I got in my car in silence, I paid the airport bill of nearly seven hundred dollars—*ouch*—and drove Patricio to his house. It was almost two in the morning, but his home was on the way.

Less than a block from his place, the streets quiet and tinged with an orange glow from the streetlamps, Patricio finally broke the silence.

"Lily, I think you should stay at my place tonight. It is a long drive to your apartment and it's very late."

Uh. No. I didn't want to create any opportunities for mixed signals. "I'll be fine." What were two more hours?

"You might be, but what about your baby?"

I blinked for a moment, letting that sink in. *Baby. Baby.* I couldn't wrap my head around it. But dammit. He was right. I had to start changing the way I lived and ate and slept and...my entire life? I was not prepared for this. Truly I wasn't.

"You can sleep in the guest room," he offered.

"What about your family?" I asked.

"They've rented a beach house—too many

to all stay with me. So you can have a bed all to yourself."

"Sure. Okay. Thanks, Patricio."

When we arrived at his house, a very adorable Mediterranean with three bedrooms and a pool, about ten miles east of Santa Monica pier, I felt ready to crash.

He came from his room and handed me an oversized T-shirt.

"Thank you, Patricio. And I'm sorry about everything." The situation had turned into a dramatic cluster fuck.

He raised his hand to my cheek. "I would go to the ends of the earth for you, Lily. What's a five-hour flight to Chicago and getting punched a few times?"

I smiled shallowly. "Thank you."

He grinned, and I noticed him looking at my lips. I felt tired and heartbroken and would love nothing more than to be held, but it would be ridiculous to consider doing anything other than licking my wounds and sorting out my life. I had to send the right signal.

"Good night, Patricio. I'll say goodbye before I leave in the morning." I planned to get up, drive home, and...I didn't know, really. I guess I'd open my shop and...

Sleep. You need sleep. Then you can figure it all out tomorrow.

"Good night." He went his way, and I went

into the bedroom and crashed the moment my head hit the pillow.

The next morning, I awoke to the strange sensation of someone watching me. Slowly, I opened my eyes and found a tiny, plump woman, with dark hair in a braid, staring down at me.

She smiled with a twinkle in her bright green eyes. "Leely!"

I sat up, wanting to ask who she was, but instead said, "Uhhhh...I'm going to throw up."

I sprang from the bed and dashed the short distance to the bathroom down the hall. I barely made it. There wasn't much in there, but my stomach didn't seem to care.

The woman appeared with a cool washcloth and placed it on the back of my neck.

"I help you up," she said with a thick Italian accent and grabbed my elbow.

Once to my feet, she guided me over to the sink and turned on the water so I could rinse my mouth and wash my face.

"Thank you."

"It is nothing, Leely. We are like-a family now."

My brain finally made the connection. "You're Patricio's mother."

"Yes. And it is very nice to meet you." She gave me a quick hug. "I will see you in the kitchen, *si*? I make the good strong breakfast for you." She flexed her arm to show me the muscle-building powers of her cooking.

"*Si*. Thank you."

She left me there to finish cleaning up, and when I got to the kitchen, Patricio's mother was yelling at him, shaking her fist in his face. Two men, one older and one younger, who both looked very much like Patricio, sat at his kitchen table, sipping coffee and watching Patricio go at it with his mother.

I didn't have the stomach for more fighting, so I slowly stepped back. Sadly, his mother noticed me.

"Leely! Come in. I make you the breakfast."

"No. It's okay. Really. I'm not hungry, and I need to get to Santa Barbara."

"Can we talk for a moment, Lily?" Patricio asked.

"Sure." I followed him into his bedroom, which was decorated in a strange ode to Hollywood style with black-and-white photos of old movie stars—James Dean, Marilyn Monroe, Humphrey Bogart.

He closed the door and shook his head. "I am very sorry, Lily. I did not expect my mother so early today. We have plans to do sightseeing."

"It's okay, but I really have to go."

"That is the thing. I told my mother this, and she got very upset that you are not with us today."

I rolled my eyes. "Patricio, I'm sorry. Your mother seems like a very nice lady, but I've got to go." And she was pretty dang low on my list of worries. Besides, I'd already figured out that the whole thing to get me to come and meet his family was more about him winning me back versus helping him out. Was his mother even sick? Who knew?

"You cannot, Lily. Now she knows you're pregnant, and now she is more upset because I did not tell her, and we are not married."

"Oh. My. God. Patricio, are you hearing yourself right now? I cannot have my life revolve around your lies." It was ridiculous. "You either tell her right now that we broke up, or I will. Either way, you can't have her believing we're still a thing and that I'm pregnant with your child. That's ridiculous, not to mention cruel."

Patricio scratched his chin. "I know you are right. I do. And I will tell her, but now is not the time, Lily. I know my mother, and just like your heart is broken, this will break hers. She deserves better."

Oh Jeez. Why did he have to love his mommy so much, and why did I have to think it was so sweet? That being said, "Look, I know you wanted me to come here and meet everyone so that I might change my mind about us, but you need to believe me when I say that I'm not ready for a relationship. I never should've started dating you to begin with."

"So you lied when you said you loved me." I watched his face flush.

What a hothead. I mean, there was passion and then there was this. Impulsive, irrational, trigger-happy with the anger. It didn't scare me, but not knowing when someone might lose their temper wasn't conducive to a peaceful, stress-free life.

Maybe it's an Italian thing. Still, it wasn't a Lily thing.

"I think I loved the idea of us becoming more. I loved our friendship. I loved how you made me laugh and how we had so much fun together." It had been easy with Patricio, and I suppose after having endured something so not-easy with Max I didn't want to take any real risks with my heart again. Nevertheless... "Everything I said to you was true, and there was a moment that I could've seen us happy if we gave our friendship time to grow."

"And now?"

"You know about now." Max had kicked me to the curb. I was pregnant. I'd been arrested for punching his mother—the horror-show mascot—and I had no clue where my business stood. Max had bought my building and put it in my name so while that saved me from an immediate catastrophe, I couldn't and wouldn't accept charity from him. I either stood on my own two feet or I didn't. *Yeah, but now you'll have someone else depending on you.*

Christ. I lowered my head into my palms and groaned. "My life is a mess."

Patricio placed his hands on my arms and squeezed gently. "It doesn't have to be. I still love you, Lily. I don't care if you were with him. All right, *si*. I do care, but I can let it go if I had you. Please do not give up on us."

Shit. Shit. Shit.

"I can't think about this right now. I really can't." Everything was so fresh and raw. I felt drunk—sad drunk, not happy drunk—with emotional uncertainty that tinged everything around me with gray.

"Fine," said Patricio. "Then think about it later. But remember that Maxwell Cole has shown you who he is and what he's made of."

And Patricio had shown me what he was made of. I mean, the guy called me a whore and wouldn't even give me the benefit of the doubt. He wouldn't return my calls, he'd lied to his family, and now he wanted to talk reconciliation?

Both men had an ugly side, and I couldn't

accept either of what I'd just seen.

"I should go now," I said.

"Stay for breakfast? You do not want to miss my mother's fresh hot chocolate. Please. And then I won't bother you again."

My mouth watered.

"*Porfavore?*" he batted his green eyes. "If not for us, then for the baby. I'm sure it's hungry."

I narrowed my eyes. Low blow. But it worked. "Okay. I'll stay."

chapter fifteen

The rest of Patricio's family showed up shortly after he and I talked. I had to admit their banter—mostly in Italian and borderline comical when the hand gestures came into play—had given me a lift and a welcomed distraction from my dark as hell mood.

His mother, who spoke the best English out of all of them, enjoyed telling me about Patricio's pet duck when he was little. Apparently, his older brother's dog ate it, which had sparked a lifelong feud. Then she and his father squabbled about some little detail of the story, but even that made me chuckle. Everyone roasted each other, but I didn't sense any lack of love. As for breakfast, some cookie type of thing with powdered sugar and chocolate drizzled on top went perfectly with the most delicious coco ever. I seriously didn't understand how they were all of a normal weight and still ate like this.

After the end of the meal, I helped with dishes and then said my goodbyes.

"You come back tomorrow for lunch, *si*?" his mother asked as I removed my apron and folded the dishtowel while the children—ages eight to fifteen—played soccer in the yard and the men argued about what attraction to see first.

I looked at Patricio, feeling awkward.

"Lily has to work tomorrow, but she will try, Mama," Patricio interjected on my behalf.

"Then when will we see you again? We must talk about the wedding. And *soon*, eh. Very soon!" She turned and smacked Patricio's arm. I took that to mean that she wasn't happy about him knocking me up before the wedding. Of course, he hadn't knocked me up, and we weren't getting married, so I took that as my cue. "Bye, all. It was a pleasure." I scrambled out of there as fast as I could, wanting nothing more than to take a breath.

Let Patricio deal with his family and his lies. I had to worry about me now.

I didn't know what Max had to do or give up to convince his mother to drop the charges, but she had. I'd gotten the news from Mr. Krane first thing Monday morning. It would've been great to have heard from Max, too, with a great explanation for his behavior or begging forgiveness, but that didn't happen either.

A week went by and not a moment passed when I didn't think of calling or texting him. And while my aching heart wanted to deny what had happened, my aching head knew it was true. So though I didn't want to eat, I ate. Though I didn't want to get out of bed, I got out of bed. I carried on. Something about having my heart crushed by Max this time around felt vastly different than before. This time, I had someone else to think about. A tiny life who, for all I knew, was absorbing every miserable emotion I felt. But the one thing I was determined to overcome was this sense that I'd done something wrong. If I'd only been pretty enough or smart enough, maybe Max would've loved me more and wanted this. If I'd tried harder and he loved me more, he would've overcome his affliction.

Bull crap.

This time, I wasn't going to allow the mental cancer to hurt me or to be carried on to my child. I had to fight.

"Lily, so nice to see you." Dr. Monroe held open the door to her office. I instantly felt more relaxed—the walk through her garden, the smell of vanilla and cinnamon in her tiny waiting room. Peaceful.

"Thanks for making time." I took a seat in front of the window overlooking the garden, and she took her usual seat across from me.

"No thanks required. That's what I'm here for. So...what's been happening?"

I looked down at my favorite black running shoes, the ones I'd worn the first time Max and I raced each other. He'd challenged me to run against him, the prize being a business trip to Milan and a Babs Levine fashion show. I'd played dirty and won, but that weekend had ended up being so much more than a trip to Italy. It had been the beginning of something wonderful and ugly and painful and beautiful. It had been the beginning of me and Max.

"So?" Dr. Monroe prodded.

I tugged down on the hem of my gray running shorts. Yep, I totally planned to sprint right after this. "Uh, yeah. Remember when you said I needed to end things with Maxwell Cole and use my tenacity on myself?"

She smiled with affection. "I didn't say you should end things. I merely pointed out that you had not had closure. But how did everything work out?"

"Long story short, he knocked me up and ran for the hills."

Dr. Monroe's jaw dropped.

Nice. Even she's shocked.

Her dark brows shrugged. "Can you go into

more detail?"

"What more do you need to know?"

"I find it difficult to believe he simply ran away."

Oh, yeah. I kept forgetting that Max wasn't just some guy but a public figure of sorts. People had their perceptions about him, even my psychologist.

"He didn't run per se; it was more of a brisk, callus-prick-type walk."

"Lily." She held out her hands in a stop gesture. "I'm here to help you see things in a way that might be closer to reality so you can make better informed decisions. So when I say that I find it difficult to believe he walked away from you, I'm not defending his character. I'm merely commenting that I find it difficult to believe any man would walk away from you. You are a very extraordinary woman. I even find myself talking to my daughters about you—albeit confidentially—but I do talk about you."

"What do you say?"

"I find your resilience fascinating. Your loyalty and heart, too. You see the world in a way that is altruistic, but you neglect yourself in the process."

"What's that have to do with Max?"

"I only know him through you, but knowing you, I can't believe he'd simply—out of cruelty—walk away like you're hinting at. There has to be another reason."

"I can't think of one. And I can't believe you'd take his side."

"I'm not taking sides, I'm helping you see the other side. And right now, my thoughts gravitate toward the moments before your accident. You were so sure, so confident that he'd betrayed you that you lashed out at him and then nearly killed yourself."

God, what a horrible bitch! I hate you for being so right. "So I should allow him the chance to tell me what really happened and then I can castrate him and cry on your couch?"

"Exactly." She smiled.

Fair enough. "I'll tell you how it goes."

"Please do, Lily. Oh, and by the way, have you told your family the good news yet?"

I cringed. "I'm waiting for the right time." My parents' stress over the matter would only add to the fire of this chaos called my life.

"Which is when?" she asked in a frank, nonjudgmental way I very much appreciated.

"When I know what I'm going to do with my life."

"I suggest, Lily, and this is not to pressure you, but I suggest allowing them to help you figure it out. That's what family is for."

I nodded. "You're right." I was just used to dealing with everything on my own. But that needed to change. I couldn't raise a child alone, nor did I want to.

Max...goddammit, Max. Why couldn't he have just been happy? I felt like he'd robbed me of something. A life as a family.

I hadn't realized it, but that was something I'd always believed I'd have when the time came. And now that he'd taken it from me, I wanted it more than ever. If not for me, then for this baby.

"Thank you, Dr. Monroe. See you next week."

➜ ⟲

When I got home, I took a deep breath and decided it was time to call Max, like Dr. Monroe said. It went into voice mail, so I called Keri.

"Lily! Ohmygod. Where have you been?"

"I'm in California," I replied.

"You have to come back. I can't put everything off any longer and people need to get paid. There are also five different store leases we're about to lose if someone doesn't sign."

"Where's Max?"

"Gone—he took off again last week."

"Why didn't you call me?"

The awkward silence on the other end of the line made my skin crawl.

"Keri?"

She sighed. "He told me not to. He said he'd really fucked things up this time and to leave you alone—something about causing you enough damage."

Huh? "This makes no sense."

"Please, Lily. You have to come back. I gave up a great job to work here, and I can't afford to be unemployed again."

I knew I was partly to blame for her losing her job earlier this year after CC was sold.

Crap. "I don't know if I can—I mean...it's complicated, Keri."

"It's not complicated, Lily. You own this company—yes, I know about it because I helped the lawyer with some of the paperwork. This is your vision, Lily, and we're all behind you, but we need you. Max is...he's..."

"What? He's what?" *A giant jerk-faced creep?*

"I've worked for him for years," she said. "I've never seen him like this. Before he left last week he was all...broken. Completely broken."

I whooshed out a breath. Something had happened to him, but what? My gut told me it had to do with his sister. "Do you have any idea where he is? Did he take his plane anywhere?"

"He's back in Buenos Aires. He said he'd return in a day or two, but even if he did, which he didn't, he'd be in no shape to run things.

Every time I talk to him, he tells me everything will have to wait. He's a mess. Please, Lily. I'm begging you. This isn't about you and Max. It's about all of us and our families."

I groaned and then looked up at the ceiling. I was sure my mother would be happy to work at the store for another week—she seemed to love it, and she'd been having fun getting all of her friends to come by for fresh baked cookies and coffee, book club meetings, knitting lessons, and anything else she could think of to get folks to come and hang out in the store. "Seeing the store full makes more people want to come in and shop," she'd said a few days ago with a perky smile. And she'd been right. The numbers didn't lie. Of course, I had no clue where I'd land with the building, which was now tied to Max.

"Okay," I finally said. "I'll come. Can you check on a flight for—" There was a knock at my door. "Hold on, Keri." I walked over and opened it, not expecting to see the stout green-eyed woman who stood there. "Mrs. Ferrari?"

The woman's eyes looked puffy and the tip of her nose was red. She'd been crying.

"Leely, we must speak."

"Uh, sure. Come in." I lifted the phone to my ear. "Keri, I have to go, but if you can help me find a flight, that would be great."

"I've already found one while we were

talking. It leaves out of Santa Barbara in an hour."

I debated for a moment. "Sure. Okay."

"I'll text you the details—thank you, Lily. You're not only saving my ass but everyone who works here now."

"See you soon." I ended the call and turned to Mrs. Ferrari. She wore a flowery white and purple dress and had her brown and silver streaked hair pulled back into a bun. Compared to my own mother, she looked much older— more like a grandma than a mom. I guessed from the size of Patricio's family, she'd started having babies young and didn't stop until she had Patricio in her forties.

"Please have a seat." I gestured to the little couch in my living room slash dining room. "Can I get you a glass of water or some coffee?"

She sat and held out her hand. "No. No, thank you. I won't be long. I only came to speak frankly with you, from a mother's heart."

"Did you drive here by yourself?"

"Yes."

"To see me?" I ran my hand nervously over my ponytail.

"Yes."

I took a seat in the armchair. "What's going on?" From the torn-up look on her face, it couldn't be good.

"Patricio has told me about his lies."

He did? Shocking. I'd half expected him to wait until she was home or on her deathbed before he ever came clean.

I folded my hands neatly in my lap. "I see."

"Dis is why I am here, Leely. I know that my boy has his beeg head up his asshole. But he loves you, Leely. And he is a good, good boy. Do not listen to the lies these garbage people Coles tell you. They are low and despicable with no morals."

Errrr… "Did Patricio send you here to say that?"

"No!" She shook her finger at me. "He thinks I went out for a walk on the beach. His car is crap, by the way, these German things drive like lumps of butter sliding down a cold river."

Uhhh…okay. Can't say I've ever heard a car's performance described quite like that.

She continued, "But diss is beside the point, Leely." She leaned in and lowered her voice. "Did you know that Patricio's oldest brother does not belong to his father?"

*All right. Getting awkw*ard. "I wasn't aware." Patricio always spoke about his family in general terms—*"We make wine, we breed horses, my family is crazy."*

She went on, "Yes. I did not marry the man who first got me… What is it that you say in English? Knocked down?"

I tried not to smile at the appropriateness of her choice of words. I definitely felt like I'd been knocked down. Every morning, I got up and then I got down. On my knees. And talked to the monster—rarrr…ughhh…gaggg…

"You mean knocked up," I offered.

"*Si*. Knocked up. But the man I felt this passion for was not a man who could be a good father."

Oh. Now I understood where she was going. "Mrs. Ferrari—"

"Please. Call me Bibiana."

"Okay." I nodded. "Bibiana, I appreciate that you came all the way to tell me this, but I'm not sure I have the same feelings for your son as he has for me."

"I know this. I see it in your eyes, and it is why I am here. You must look forward, Leely, and see the future. Not only for you, but for your children. Do you want a husband who is broken with a broken family or do you want them to grow up loved with many people who will care for them always."

"You know the answer to that, but it's not that easy." And it wasn't as if I didn't have family of my own.

"It *is* that easy. You commit to a man. You accept his heart. And then you live. It is that easy, Leely."

She made it all sound so simple, like signing

up for cable.

She continued, "I only want you to hear from his mother's mouth that he is a good boy who loves you. He lied to me and, for this, I am upset, but it should only convince you of his good nature. He wanted to protect me and nothing more."

I drew a breath and nodded.

"*We* want you, Leely. We do not know you, but we know you are the only woman to take our Patricio's heart and make it bigger than himself. He does not care about being the real father of your baby. He only cares about loving you and being a husband to you, and this is everything."

Her words brought tears to my eyes. And it was so sweet how much she loved her son. But it changed nothing. Or did it?

No. Definitely no.

"Thank you, Bibiana. But it's like I said, the issue was never Patricio. It was always—"

There was a knock on my door.

Great. I went over and opened it. "Mom?"

"Hi, sweetie! I thought you might enjoy a little three-bean salad and a meatloaf." She moved past me and then stopped, catching sight of Bibiana. "Well, hello. I didn't realize Lily had visitors. I'm her mother, Gladys."

Bibiana stood. "It is so nice to meet you, Leely's mother. I am the mother of Patricio."

My mother set down her containers of food on my little kitchen/dining table. "Oh my god. It's so nice to meet you. Patricio is such a lovely young man."

Why did I suddenly feel like a kindergartner whose mom was meeting one of the other moms in order to set up a playdate?

Bibiana walked around my coffee table to give my mother a giant hug and a kiss on each cheek.

Once properly greeted a la Italiana, my mother pulled back. "So nice to finally meet you."

"You can call me Bibiana. We are almost like family."

My mother's stiff brows told me she was confused but trying to hide it in the name of politeness. Given I was done with the charades and juvenile game playing, I felt obligated to tell my mother why Bibiana was here. But before I could open my mouth, there was another knock at the door.

I froze with fear. The last two knockers had been these two women, and frankly, I needed to get packed and off to the airport. With a groan, I went to open the front door. "Max?"

He looked like a castaway—thick stubble, wrinkled clothes, circles under his eyes. He still looked manly and gorgeous with that tall frame and angular jaw, but it wasn't like him to look so…sloppy. Max was Mr. Perfect even on casual Fridays.

"Lily, you remember my mother, Maxine." He stepped aside and there stood…there stood…

His mother? What the fuck? She wore her dark hair perfectly straight and had on large sunglasses. A white bandage covered her nose.

Maxine leaned around him and extended her hand. "Hello, Lily," she said with a stiffness that sounded like an insult.

Stunned, I took her hand and shook it, but I looked at Max.

"May we come in?" he asked.

Fuck. Patricio's mother was inside as well as my own. Neither was a fan of Max's mother, and I was pissed and heartbroken over Max.

"Lily, I know what you must be thinking," said Max, "but just hear me out. Please."

"Uhhh…okeydokey." I stepped aside to let them pass.

The moment I shut the door and turned, I was greeted with the uncomfortable view of everyone looking at each other, glaring, but saying nothing.

This is awesome.

I clapped my hands. "All right. Let's do introductions." I gestured toward my mother. "This is Gladys, my wonderful mother. This is Bibiana," I looked at her not-happy face,

"Patricio's mother. And this is..." I tried my best not to snarl, spit, or swing with a fist at her bandaged nose, "the woman who gave birth to Max." She didn't deserve the term "mother," now did she?

"Lily..." Max growled.

"Sorry." I held up my hands. "This is Max's mother."

No one said anything.

Awkward. Awkward. More awkward...Excellent.

"All right. How nice of everyone to stop by, but I have a flight to catch," I said.

"Lily." Max grabbed my arm. "You need to hear me—"

Someone pounded on my front door.

"Well," I said with acerbic enthusiasm, "I wonder who that could be?" Perhaps the IRS or a drug gang. I mean what could possibly make this situation any more horrible?

I reached for the door. *Ah. He could.*

"Patricio." My shoulders dropped. "Why don't you come in and join the godawful party."

He cocked a brow.

"Never mind," I said, this time leaving the door wide open in case anyone else wanted to join the fun.

Patricio took one look at his mother and started berating her in Italian. I could only assume he wasn't happy about her meddling.

While those two began to rant, Max pulled me aside.

"Lily," he spoke softly, "I'm sorry for the way I behaved the other day. It was wrong to walk away from you like that."

Just seeing his face opened up the floodgates of anger. Call it hormones, call it the heartbreak speaking, but I lost it.

I looked up at his face and, without realizing what I was doing, I slapped him. Hard. His head whipped to the side.

"Wrong? Wrong! Fuck you, Max!" Wrong was the word a person used when they incorrectly cited a historical date or purchased the incorrect flavor of ice cream. *Oops, I wanted rocky road, not banana crunch. Wrong one!* Or Fidel Castro became dictator of Cuba in 1979. *Oh, sorry. That's wrong. It was 1976.* But "wrong" was the *wrong* word to describe telling the woman you supposedly love that it's "unfortunate" she's pregnant, followed by walking away from her.

"Lily!" my mother scolded.

Max placed his hand on his cheek. "I deserved that."

"Like hell you did!" his mother said. "She has no right to treat you like that. She's trash. Pure trash!"

I heard my mother gasp. I heard Patricio cuss in Italian. As for Bibiana, she said, "It is like

I told you, Lily. They are monsters."

"Monsters?" Max's mother seethed. "That's rich coming from a woman who pumps out illiterate rapists and thugs by the dozen."

"You dare insult my mother?" Patricio yelled and stepped toward Maxine.

Max stepped between them. "Back the fuck off, Patricio. She may be a horrible bitch, but she's still my mother."

I suddenly forgot what I wanted to say as my mind reeled with that little gem.

Max quickly looked at me. "Lily, can we talk in private? I need to tell you—"

"No. I'm done with the games. So say what you have to say and then leave," I replied.

"Fine." He looked down at his polished black shoes for a moment. "My sister's baby did not make it."

Oh no. My heart felt heavier and the room fell silent.

"When I came back to Chicago that night, I'd come back to get my mother. Mabel was getting closer to dying and wouldn't give the doctors permission to induce labor. She said she would be a horrible mother and, if anyone deserved to live, it was her child."

I blinked waiting to hear the rest, but not really wanting to.

"I flew my mother down to talk some sense into Mabel and to say what was long overdue."

My eyes teared. I could only imagine the sort of painful emotions Max had to go through to turn to his mother for help. He'd sacrificed a lot to extract her from his life.

"But I'm sorry, Lily. I truly am. I love you so much, and the only thing I could think when you said you were pregnant was that something might happen to you. I didn't know how to deal with that and everything else."

Somewhere in the middle of Max's speech, I heard a loud gasp coming from my mother's direction.

"You're pregnant?" she asked.

I slowly looked at her, wincing. "I'm sorry. I was going to tell you."

For the first time in a very long time, I saw my mother bubble with rage. *Jesus. She's going to tear me a new one.*

I held up my finger. "Hold that thought, Mom." I reached for Max's hand. "I'm so, so sorry you went through that, but you should've told me. You should've said something."

"Yes. I should've, but I hadn't slept in days, and watching my sister slowly withering and—I wasn't thinking straight. Nor did I have the luxury of time to argue with you over my choice to invite my mother back into my life..." His voice trailed off as he shook his head.

I could see how that might be difficult given she'd baited me into a fight and had me arrested.

"Maybe I wouldn't have understood, Max, but you didn't give me the chance and then you turned your back on me like that?" I whooshed out a breath.

"It is who they are," said Bibiana. "The Coles do not care who they hurt."

Maxine whipped off her glasses. "I should say the same for you. Your disgusting son took advantage of my daughter. She was only sixteen."

I looked at Patricio. I knew he'd been eighteen or nineteen when he'd slept with Mabel. I couldn't claim his actions to be horrific or evil—teenagers are, after all, not the brightest lights at the disco—but he had apparently broken the girl's heart.

"Apologize," I said to Patricio.

He gave me a shocked look as if he did not understand.

"You heard me. Apologize to them." I indicated Max and Maxine.

Patricio's eyes shifted around the room. "But I—"

"He will not apologize!" Bibiana seethed. "That girl was a slut."

"What?" Maxine snapped.

"Okay. Now *you* have to apologize." I pointed to Bibiana. "That was out of line. How would you like it if someone called one of your daughters that because she had sex. Unmarried." I zeroed in on Bibiana with my eyes. She'd told me ten minutes earlier that she'd slept with some man and then married Patricio's father.

Bibiana got my gist and snapped her mouth shut. She looked down at the ground. "I am sorry."

"Now your turn," I prodded Patricio. "Tell them you're sorry for causing their family any pain."

Patricio's mouth flapped a little.

"You might be a dad someday. Think about how you'd feel if Mabel had been your daughter."

Patricio looked up. "Fine. I am sorry for touching your daughter."

I could see that Max wasn't going to let it go. He had hate written all over his face.

"Max, tell Patricio that you're sorry for beating the crap out of him. Twice."

Max folded his arms over his chest. "I'm not sorry. He deserved it."

I let out a breath. "But you should be, Max. Because if you can't see that almost killing someone—someone's son, by the way— because you're upset is wrong, then you're not really the man I thought you were. Honestly, what kind of father will you be?"

Max's hazel eyes narrowed on my face. "I'm

sorry for almost killing you." He glanced at Patricio, and Patricio answered with a nod.

I knew these two families would never like each other, but I felt good knowing that they now had a chance to move on. Even better, they might leave my apartment.

"Okay. So, thank you, everyone," I said. "But I have to—"

"Uh-uh, young lady," my mother seethed. "I think you're missing someone."

Goddaaaammit. I really just wanted them to go. I needed to be alone with Max because he still had a hell of a lot of explaining to do. I mean, yeah, I understood that Max didn't think like a normal guy, and he often did ridiculous and strange things, such as waiting for the right moment to address an issue, but he couldn't do this to me anymore. He couldn't put me on hold and leave me hanging until everything was perfect or he had just the right words for whatever apology. Life was messy! And if he wanted to be a part of mine, he had to be there for me. He had to tell me what the hell was going on, not shut me out!

Uhhh...you should talk, Miss "I'll tell you I'm pregnant later, Mom."

Dammit. Look at me calling the kettle black.

I slowly turned to my mother, feeling the sting of shame. "I'm sorry, Mom, for not telling you I'm pregnant."

She crossed her arms. "And whose baby is it?"

"Max's," I replied.

My mother's eyes snapped to his face like she just might kill him.

"Sorry?" he said.

"You just wait, young man," my mother shook her finger at him, "until Lily's father hears about this."

"Okay, Mom—everyone!—that's enough," I said. "You all need to go now."

"We're not done yet," said Max. "One more person in this room needs to apologize. Make that two, since, as you've pointed out, Lily, kicking the crap out of people isn't the way to handle your anger."

Oh. Yeah. I had punched his mother. I'd sorta forgotten about that. I almost laughed. I had put myself up there on a pedestal. But leave it to Max to set me straight. He was good at that, always telling me like it was. Ugly truth or beautiful truth. I could depend on him to give it.

"You're right." I nodded and looked at Maxine. "I'm sorry for breaking your nose." *But I secretly hope it heals crooked and serves as a constant reminder of your general horribleness.*

Maxine stared with those cold hazel eyes.

"Mother?" Max warned. "We have an agreement. You want to be a part of our lives, you will apologize. You will get help. You will not hurt us or Lily anymore. It's now or never. Die alone or change. Because we're done taking your sick bullshit."

She regarded him for a moment and then drew a breath, but no words came out.

"You made a promise to Mabel," he growled. "You made a promise to me. So while Dad will never come back, you still have a chance to make things right with us."

Max's father finally left Maxine? That was news. According to Max, his father had been afraid of the woman and never stood up to her, even for his children's sake.

Maxine cleared her throat and looked at me. "I'm sorry for the pain I've caused you and your family, Lily."

"And?" Max growled. I had to say that seeing him like this, refusing to allow her even an inch of control over him, felt inspiring. His mother's disorder had controlled, ruined, tainted, damaged, deformed, and maimed his life. When I'd met him, he was beginning to really take back what was stolen from him. Perhaps breaking ties with his mother and dissolving Cole Cosmetics had been necessary to start fresh. Either way, Max was no longer taking her shit in any form.

"Well?" he warned his mother.

She sighed. "I'm sorry for having naked

photos of you published and for the part I played in ruining your relationship with my son."

"And?" Max urged.

There was more? I kind of felt like we should quit while we were ahead.

"And I promise that I will get help for my disorder so that I can someday be a part of your lives."

Oh. So that was what this was about? She wanted to be a part of my baby's life. *Hell no!* My knee-jerk reaction, to ensure she disappeared down a deep, dark well, melted away as I saw her eyes begin to tear. There it was again—that look in her eyes that told me she hated herself more than anyone in this room could possibly hate her.

"I, uhh…" I didn't have the right words.

My mother stepped in. "When you're ready, the door will be open."

That had been a bit too generous. I would've gone for something more like, *We'll not spit in your face when you enter a room.*

I flashed a disapproving look at my mother.

My mother shrugged. "She just lost her only grandchild. Have a little heart, Lily."

Okay. Now I was back to feeling guilty again. *Dammit!* Why couldn't I pick an emotion and stick with it? Everything was so complicated.

"Thank you," Maxine said humbly.

I bobbed my head, feeling thoroughly ransacked on an emotional level. So, true to my nature, I turned my focus to work. Max obviously had a horrible family situation to deal with, the employees at LLL were about to lose their shirts if someone didn't step up, and I needed to get everyone the hell out of my apartment so I could catch a breath and talk to Max. There was much to discuss, but the more immediate issue was the sinking LLL ship.

I was about to politely ask everyone to leave, except for Max, when Patricio's mother chimed in.

"Then there is only one last thing to settle," Bibiana stated.

"Which is?" I asked.

"Who are you going to marry?" she asked with a sharp tone.

My mouth dropped open. It was pretty uncool of her to put me on the spot like that, especially since everyone already knew the answer. Patricio didn't deserve to have the knife twisted in his heart.

I glanced at Patricio, expecting him to step in and tell his mother that now was not the time, but I found him staring at me expectantly. He crossed his arms over his chest.

I looked at Max for help, but found him looking down at me with a cocked eyebrow as if to say, *Well? We're waiting.*

I glanced at my mother, and even she had a look of eager anticipation in her eyes. "Lily," my mother scorned, "you are pregnant. And everyone in this room is emotionally vested in this. You will settle this right now so everyone can get on with their lives."

"Exactly," Max said. "If you're planning on marrying someone else, I'd rather know now. Either way, I plan on being a part of the baby's life."

I went back to looking at the two men, realizing they still believed they were competing to marry me. Not true. I saw Patricio more as a friend, which I'd already told him. In my mind the question was about whether I could move forward with Max. So really what I saw were two different choices, two different lives I could live. One, without Max, would probably mean I'd eventually settle down with someone like Patricio, someone I felt safe and comfortable with, but did not love in that all-consuming, terrifying kind of way because there could only be one Max. I'd stick with my shop, raise my child alone and probably be just fine. A life with Max meant taking a giant leap of faith. A life with him terrified me.

What terrifies you is losing him again. Or what if he simply got tired of me? I wouldn't survive another heartbreak like that.

I groaned and rubbed my hands over my face. I had to stop allowing that fugly voice to fill my head with doubts. Max did love me. He had made mistakes, but so had I. And everything he'd done since we'd met showed me he'd never wanted anyone like he wanted me, and that included when my face looked so unattractive that not a single man had ever touched me. He'd seen beyond my appearance and fell in love with *me*. The real *me*.

Ha! Fuck you, fugly. I win.

I lifted my chin, turned to face Max, and smiled. "I choose you. But I'm not ready to get married." There was all of this emotional rubble in the way and it would take time to clear it out.

Max's expression turned all gooey warm. "I love you, Lily. You have no idea. And we can definitely discuss marriage later in a more private setting." Max smiled, and I knew the look in his eyes meant he was not going to let me off the hook so easily.

And he can sell ice to an Eskimo. I sighed. I did love him. So much it hurt.

"You are really choosing that son of a bitch over me?" Patricio growled.

Uh-oh. Here we go again. I prepared to step between them, but when I looked at Max, I realized I wouldn't have to. He was perfectly calm.

My man.

"Patricio!" his mother barked. "Leely has made her choice, and you will take it like a grown man." His mother dipped her head. "It was a pleasure meeting you, Leely. I wish you both much happiness. Come, son." She marched out and Patricio followed, but right as he reached the door, he looked back at me with sheer hate in his eyes.

A shiver washed over me.

"You just made a very big mistake, Lily." He left, and I felt the tension I'd been holding in my body begin to release.

Funny, I'd never realized that. Whenever I was around Patricio or thinking about being with him, my stomach got all knotted up. It had been him the entire time—or, more accurately stated, I'd known all along that he wasn't the one for me. I'd tried to ignore it but couldn't. My heart knew. And so did my stomach.

"Well," my mother said with a displeased tone, "I'm guessing that this is my cue and that you need someone to look after the store today."

"Thank you, Mom. And I am sorry for not telling you. I just didn't want to worry you."

Her eyes filled with tears, but I couldn't tell if they were tears of joy or sorrow. She then walked over and gave me a giant hug.

"I never liked Patricio anyway," she

whispered. "There's something off about him." She turned to Max and gave him a hug, standing up on her tiptoes since she was short like me and didn't want her face smooshed into his pecs. "Congratulations, Max. You're going to make a great father."

"Thank you, Gladys." He smiled. "I only hope I can make Lily happy, like she deserves."

My mother glowed with that remark. "Call me later and let me know what the plan is."

"Bye, Mom," I said.

"Mother," said Max, "Lily and I have a few things to discuss. Callahan will take you to the airport. You can take my jet."

"Aren't you coming back to Chicago?" She sounded a little naggy, like she didn't approve of him staying here with me.

He gave her a stern look.

"See you back in Chicago." She disappeared out the door.

"Finally, we're alone." Max walked over to the door, closed it, and turned the lock. He faced me with a very hard look in his eyes. "Now you and I are going to talk."

Oh goodie. More drama. Just what I was hoping for.

I crossed my arms over my chest. "About what?"

His eyes flickered with annoyance. "What do you mean you don't want to get married?"

he growled and reached for the top button of his pants.

I smiled. *Get ready to buy some ice, Lily.*

chapter sixteen

Max wasted absolutely no time in getting my running shoes off, my shorts down, and me up against the wall. I'd heard people talk about makeup sex before, but until he thrust himself into me, burying his cock as far as my body would allow, I didn't fully understand. Now I did.

Holding me up by the legs, he slid out, leaving only the tip of his shaft inside me, and then slammed into me again. I let out a soft moan as his thickness and length rubbed against my inner walls with a forcefulness that I hadn't seen from him before.

At first it was a shock, feeling him hammer into me like that, angry or something. But with each stroke of his hard cock, I felt what he felt. So much emotion had built up inside me, I needed to let it out. I needed to let go. Because, dammit, I was still really pissed about how he'd taken the news of my pregnancy.

Angry sex rocks.

"Harder, Max." I gripped his shoulders, pushing my body into him while he fucked me. I gasped and panted, trying not to come as the tip of his head repeatedly drove against that throbbing spot deep inside. Instead, I focused on the feel of him entering my body, driving his emotions and lust into me with every angry thrust.

He withdrew and lowered my feet to the floor. "I want to look at all of you. I love looking at you." He tore my shirt over my head. I unclasped my bra to move things along while he ripped off his shirt.

His eyes took me in, starting at my toes, moving up my thighs to the cleft between my legs, and then to my breasts. "God, I love those tits."

He pulled me into him and lifted me again. With my arms around his neck and our mouths locked in a frenzy of hot needy kisses, he carried me to the bedroom and lowered me onto the bed. The moment my body hit the mattress, he drove his cock deep into my body.

I gasped with pleasure. *Holy hell.* He felt so good.

I moved my hands down his muscular back, enjoying the feel of his heavy body pushing me down and his smooth skin under my palms.

Pistoning his hips at a furious pace, he

threaded his fingers with mine. "You're mine, Lily. Say it. Say you're mine."

With his dick inside me and my c-spot on the verge of sending me shooting off like a rocket, I knew this was the moment he was waiting for: Me at his mercy.

"Say it," he repeated with a deliciously forceful thrust of his thick shaft.

"I'm yours," I panted my words.

"Say it again." He drove into me, deeper this time.

Oh God. Almost there. Almost there. "I'm yours," I moaned my words.

"We're getting married next week."

Huh?

"Say it," he demanded.

At that exact same moment, his cock hit that magical spot deep inside me and his pelvis hit my c-spot. Every nerve ending exploded with crippling ecstasy and radiated out to every limb all the way to the tips of my toes and fingers. "Yes. Oh, God. Yes."

He worked his shaft with just the right amount of pressure, extracting wave after wave of contractions. I couldn't see straight. My nails dug into his shoulders.

He grunted with his release and pumped his cum inside me, triggering one more sensual wave of my own release.

At that moment, all I knew was that having

our bodies tangled together, the sound of his deep masculine voice flowing through my ears, the delicious scent of his fresh sweat and expensive cologne permeating my nose, would be the one thing in my life I could never get enough of. There was no replacement for him, for this, for us.

Several long moments passed before Max dropped his head on my shoulder, letting out a long breath.

"Wow. That was...intense," I muttered, still enjoying the feel of him inside me and of us together.

"It's only going to get better." He lifted his head and looked at me. "You know that, don't you?"

It took a moment for me to realize that he wasn't talking about sex. He was talking about us. And probably him. Maybe even me.

I brushed the hair from his forehead and stared at him. He was so beautiful. Now more than ever.

"Yeah," I said softly, "I know."

"Good." He pulled out, got up from the bed, and swiped his jeans from the floor. He returned and looked down at me. "Because I meant what I said. We are getting married next week."

"What's the hurry?" I had enough to worry about.

He kneeled beside the bed, planted his elbows next to me, and held out a small black box. "Lily, you need to know I'm in it with you one hundred percent. I won't ever turn my back on you again. I won't ever shut you out again. Even if it's not easy and humiliating for me, I won't hide from you when I feel afraid." He opened the box and revealed a ridiculously large engagement ring.

"You're proposing. Naked?" I sat up, still naked myself.

"Seems appropriate, don't you think?" He flashed his trademark, charming smile that displayed his dimples and made his eyes light up. I could look at that smile the rest of my life and never tire of it.

"The naked part is wonderful. And so is that ring." It had a huge princess-cut stone surrounded by tiny diamonds, giving it a vintage feel. "But we don't need to get married."

"Uh-uh. I'm not taking any more chances, Lily. I am not risking losing you again." He slid the ring from the case, grabbed my left hand, and slid it effortlessly onto my ring finger.

"It's perfect," I said with a sigh.

He kissed the top of my hand. "Exactly like you, Lily."

I smiled and leaned in to kiss him. "I love you, Max."

"I hope so. Because I am never letting go of you again."

∿ ∿

After our little—okay, very unlittle—romp, Max and I took a shower, ate, and then called Keri to let her know we'd both be flying back to Chicago that evening on the red-eye. She was ecstatic, of course, because everyone at LLL had been busting their asses to get the company up and running. But when Max took the phone and told Keri he needed help getting a wedding booked for next weekend, here in Santa Barbara, Keri went ape-shit happy. I could hear the shrieking from three feet away.

"Nothing big or fancy, Keri. I want small, quiet, no press. Got it?" He grinned at me and then ended the call. "I hope that's okay?"

"You have no idea how badly I do not want a big fussy wedding. Thank you."

He stepped closer and wrapped his arms around my waist. "You sure? Because I'm ready to give you anything you want."

"I've got you. That's more than enough."

"And in about eight months, we are going to have someone new to love," he said.

"Life is completely surreal."

He pinched my chin and tipped my head up. "Just remember, Lily, whatever happens from here on out, we're in it together—good, bad, ugly."

I stared up into his eyes. "Are you worried?"

"I won't lie. Yes."

"But I'm sure you'll keep your disorder in check. Look how far you've come."

"I'm not worried about me," he said. "I'm worried about you."

"Why?"

"Because I know you. And I know how hard it is for you to accept that you truly deserve the good things in your life—including us."

I nodded, understanding where he was coming from. "Well, every journey starts with one step, and today I stepped toward you." I smiled, feeling like through all of this drama and emotional pain, I'd taken a part of me back and diminished the power that ugly voice had over me. "I'm just not ready to step toward your mother. She's scary."

Max chuckled. "Not to worry. She knows she can't be a part of our life in any way until we're convinced she belongs there. We've got a long way to go."

I wasn't so sure I'd ever want her in my life, but seeing Max take control of this very difficult part of his past made me proud. And I guess it inspired me a little, too. It took a lot of strength to confront one's fears. Especially for Max, who never even wanted to admit when he felt afraid. It was too imperfect in his mind to feel anything but confident. I think that was maybe why he'd retreated when I told him I was pregnant. He'd felt ashamed to show me anything but strength, something he couldn't do after watching his sister lose her baby and almost die.

Well, with time, he'd get used to the fact that I didn't need him to be perfect. I only needed him to be there.

Max glanced at his watch. "You and I have a company to build and a plane to catch."

I grabbed my suitcase filled with clothes I'd shoved inside. I'd have to go shopping later because I did not have the right wardrobe for this new role I'd be taking on.

"Hey, by the way, how much money am I going to pay myself?" I asked.

"Nothing." He grabbed one of my suitcases.

I lifted a brow. "Nothing? I have to make some money."

He laughed.

"What's so funny?" I asked.

"You're marrying me." He opened the front door to my apartment.

"I'm not going to sponge off of you. That's weird."

He shook his head as I passed him, wheeling my second suitcase.

He closed the door. "I see we're going to

have to work on your idea of marriage, Miss Snow."

"Ha. Okay, Mr. Cole."

"Starting with taking up one residence and getting rid of your revolting furniture."

"Oh, we're so keeping my thrift-store gems. We'll put them in the nursery." I was joking of course, but watching Max hold back his urge to retch was priceless.

"If it makes you happy, Lily. Then I'm all in."

chapter seventeen

The next week, Max and I worked long hours—
me not as much as him because he insisted I
rest a little more than usual. Still, we managed
to get up early, run together, which we loved,
and put some very productive hours in at the
office, including very hot sex over my awesome
new desk at lunchtime. Honestly, I didn't know
if it was the hormones, the new vitamins I was
taking, or simply the bliss of feeling like my life
was in a good place with the man I loved, but I
just couldn't get enough of him. If I were a
dude, I would've been walking around with a
baseball-bat-sized erection in my pants all day
long.

Thankfully, being the manly stud that Max
was, he didn't mind one bit, helping me with
my endless sexual need. He was ready to serve
selflessly.

"Yes, hard, *hard* work, keeping you
satisfied, Lily," as he'd say.

Anyway, we still managed to get the leases signed, materials ordered for the new locations, and have meetings with key retailers—ones who would carry our merchandise in strategic cities where we did not plan to open stores of our own. I spoke to my mother about running Lily's Pad, and she had the great idea of adding LLL's products, too. "Are you sure, Mom? I mean running a store is a lot of work," I'd said. "Now you want to run two stores in one?"

"Honey, I spent most of my life taking care of you guys. For the first time, I'm doing something I enjoy for me. Of course, I do want a raise and we need to hire part-time help, but I wouldn't dream of letting my shop go."

How cute, I'd thought. She'd called it her shop. I supposed now it was. "You got it, Mom. See you Saturday."

"Oh, I can't believe you're getting married on Sunday," she'd squealed. "And I can't wait to show everyone pictures."

"Mom, you didn't tell anyone, did you?"

"No. Of course not. Just the girls."

Oh crap. That was something like twenty people. And possibly every person who entered the store.

"Mom! It's supposed to be a secret."

"Oh, now. They won't tell a soul."

Those women gossiped so much, they put tabloids to shame. "I guess it's too late to do anything about it."

"Oh, you're such a worrywart," she said.

Me? The queen of worrying had called me a worrywart? *Wow, times really are changing.*

She continued, "It's going to be wonderful, Lily. You just focus on your special day with friends and family."

In all, we'd invited only eighteen people—my immediate family; two of my good friends, who I'd known since elementary school, and their plus ones; and Danny and Calvin. From Max's side, he had invited his father (we weren't ready for his mother); Keri and her boyfriend; and a few friends of his—one of them who I knew well: Mark Douglas. Mark had also been my mentor in college and was the person who'd recommended me for a job at CC. Max also invited his sister, but we both knew she wasn't quite in the best of shape to travel. We'd promised to visit her in a month or so, but Max spoke to her every day and threatened regularly to make her move back to the States. She'd said she might consider it but needed time. I knew Max would eventually persuade her because he always got his way and seemed genuinely excited to have her back in his life. Now that he'd begun thinking about family, I knew part of him wouldn't feel content until she and her husband were a part of ours.

As for the wedding, I'll be honest. When I

was little, I'd dreamt of the big to-do, but now, simply having Max felt big enough. The rest of the church could be empty, and I'd be on cloud nine.

"See you in a few days, Mom. And no more telling."

Of course, that hadn't happened. The next day, we began seeing articles pop up in the tabloids (Keri kept an eye on that for us), and the vultures began circling outside the LLL building.

By Friday night, we had a swarm of them outside Max's home when we pulled up in the town car with Callahan at the wheel.

"They won't go inside, will they?" I asked.

"No, Lily." Max patted my hand. "They know they cannot trespass."

"But why are they even here? Who gives a crap about us getting married other than us?"

Max nodded. "Apparently enough people that these photographers feel it necessary to stalk us everywhere we go." He gave me a reassuring look. "Don't worry. They'll move on in a few days. I promise."

The car pulled forward, passed the gate, and we headed inside.

"You hungry?" Max asked, loosening his red silk tie while I kicked off my black heels right in the foyer.

"Yes. But not for food." My eyes washed

over his body. I wanted nothing more than to rip his gray dress shirt and those very expensive-looking slacks from his tight body.

"Well, I suppose we could get a little fucking in before eating." He approached me and pulled me into his arms. Then he froze.

"What's wrong?"

"This is our last night together as single people."

"You're single?" I scowled. Because I sure the hell wasn't.

"I merely meant unmarried."

"In that case, I suppose you're right, but what's a wedding when you've got someone's seed growing inside you?"

He made a sour face. "Seed?"

"That really is a horrible thing to call a baby, isn't it?"

"It's barbaric." He leaned down and kissed me. "Just like the things I'm going to do to you in exactly two minutes."

"Barbaric, huh?" I liked the sound of that.

"You are carrying my child, so we can dial it down to barbaric light. Only a bit of spanking and nipple pinching."

"I suppose I can make that happen." I reached out and tweaked his nipple through his shirt.

"Uh-uh. Mr. Cole doesn't play that." He swatted my hand away and laughed.

"I'm not sure I like your tone, Mr. Cole. What's good for the goose, and all that…"

He shook his head, reached for my arm, and bent at the knees, tugging me towards him. He didn't slam me over his shoulder, but at the same time, I couldn't wiggle away.

Before I knew it, he was carrying me up the stairs.

"Hey!" I protested.

He yanked up my favorite brown skirt and smacked me hard on the ass. "Shut up. You're not allowed to speak."

I couldn't see his face, but I heard the smile. "Ha. Ha. Funny, Mr. Cole."

We reached his—I mean *our*—bedroom, and he lowered me to my feet.

I looked up at him. "I hope you're ready for some hot nipple action." I made little crab claws with my hands.

He pushed me back into the bed. "It's our last night together before the wedding. The only thing I'm planning on is fucking you senseless so there's no chance of you getting cold feet."

I propped myself up on my elbows. "You think I'm going to get cold feet?"

"I know you will, Lily. And I know that marrying me is a huge leap of faith. But I believe in us, and I know you won't fuck it up this time."

I almost felt like getting angry, but he and I had always been brutally honest with each other. It was the foundation of our relationship. "No. I won't fuck it up this time."

"Good." He slid his hand up inside my skirt and tugged down my black panties. "Now be quiet while I get to work."

I grinned at his playful alpha talk. I loved this man. I loved him more than anything. Which was why I'd allow him to think he was in charge.

At least for one more night.

The wedding would be a simple ceremony in a nondenominational church right down the street from the small beachside restaurant where we'd have our reception dinner. I loved the sound of everything being quiet and intimate. Just our closest friends coming for a nice meal while we laughed, ate, and watched the sun go down. I mentally blocked out the fact some press would be lurking outside. I would simply pretend they didn't exist. Nothing would ruin this day. Because when I stepped back and reflected, the fact that this man, whom I loved so much, loved me back, well...I still couldn't quite believe it. Not that I didn't have anything to offer him, but he literally could have almost anyone. Hot model, gorgeous actresses—pretty much anyone with a pulse who was into men would at the very least consider him.

"Please, stop staring. It's making me feel self-conscious," Max said with a grin from the seat next to me as his private plane touched down in the small Santa Barbara airport. I tried not to let this lifestyle go to my head. None of it was really important at the end of the day.

"Sorry, I can't help it. None of this feels real." By tomorrow evening, we'd be husband and wife. Maxwell Cole and Lily Snow. My ex-boss and the girl who'd never had a kiss until she met him.

He ran his thumb over my bottom lip, beaming at my face. "No, it does not."

"How did you see yourself getting married? In a big church in Italy or on a yacht?"

He chuckled. "What in the world makes you think I ever wanted to get married?"

Oh. "You didn't?"

"No. I had my company to keep me occupied."

"And you had women like Adeline to keep your bed warm," I said.

He made a noncommittal shrug. "I was a declared bachelor and had no interest in anything serious with anyone. Least of all Adeline. But then I met you, Lily."

His words made me feel all toasty and gooey inside.

He continued, "I'm not sure the exact moment it happened, but I realized that life could be better with you in it. I could be successful and happy." He shook his head. "I never thought happiness would be in the cards for me. There was only moving forward." He kissed me, and the velvety softness of his lips made me melt.

Then it made me super horny.

I leaned into him, deepening the kiss. I placed my hand on his thigh and slowly ran it up to his groin, where I found a very hard and long something wonderful.

He pushed my hand away and broke the kiss. "Uh-uh. Not until the wedding night."

"What?" I protested. "Who set up that rule?"

"I did. Otherwise, I doubt we'll ever get through the actual ceremony. Or the dinner."

"Come on. The bathroom's right there." I pointed to the teeny room. "We can totally fit."

Meanwhile the plane had completely stopped.

Max unfastened his seatbelt and adjusted himself. I could only stare hopelessly at the magnificent part of his body he'd just denied me.

"So I'll see you tomorrow, then?" He pulled

my carry-on out of a small closet near the front exit and set it down.

"Yes." I pouted. "And tell Mark no hookers, strippers, or too much scotch. I need you disease-free and hangover-free tomorrow." Mark Douglas, the guy who had been my mentor and was Max's friend, had planned some sort of private bachelor party thing at a posh club in L.A.

I stood and walked over to Max, taking one last look at him. He was so beautiful, more now than ever because I loved him so much.

"All right now." He scooted me toward the door, which had been opened up by the copilot.

I suddenly felt nervous, my stomach knotting, my pulse racing, my brain scrambling to keep me from feeling like something was going to go wrong.

"What?" Max gripped my shoulders, probably noticing my extremely pale face.

I took a breath and closed my eyes. *Breathe, breathe, breathe.* The sensation started to subside. "Nothing, just a little woozy from the flight, I think?" I made a little circle on my stomach.

"You sure? I'll cancel the party if you need me to stay."

How sweet. "No. I'm good. I promise." I stepped toward the door, doing my best to hide what was really going on. Horror. Crippling horror. That voice inside my head telling me that something would get in our way, that I'd ruin it. I didn't deserve him, and sooner or later, he'd come to realize it, leaving me with nothing but a giant broken heart.

Stop it. Cold feet, you idiot. Perfectly normal. I went to my tiptoes and gave Max a peck on the lips. "I love you, Mr. Cole. Have fun tonight, but not too much fun." I winked and descended the staircase.

"I love you, too," he called out. "No getting arrested, Miss Snow!"

"Har har." I was going to my parents' house for the night. Danny was already here in town with Calvin, though he wasn't invited. Girls only. Okay, except for my dad, who planned to hide in his room, watching a game. My longtime childhood friends Kate and Nell were coming over, along with a few of my mother's best friends, who were more like her sisters. We'd planned to do floral arrangements, play a few games—they were going to drink champagne, I was not—and watch some movies—*The Proposal* or *Maid of Honor*—chick-flick stuff.

I waved at Max and smiled. There was this moment where I think he realized that my smile was a lie, but I turned and headed for the parking lot, where my mom was waiting to pick me up.

I heard the door of the plane close and the engines start up.

Everything will be fine, Lily. Everything will be fine as long as you don't fuck it up.

chapter eighteen

"Lily, you look absolutely gorgeous." The next morning, my mother preened over the white veil stuck to the tight bun on the back of my head while I finished my makeup. Today, I felt like a princess. I woke up late after a long night of girl-fun, the best part being watching them get hammered and act like total idiots, including my mother, who decided to show us dance moves from the seventies.

We'd finished up tying the ribbons on the floral arrangements we'd all made last night, and my father had taken them over to the church this morning.

I texted Max, but didn't hear back from him until one-ish.

> **Me:** *how'd it go last night? Any unusual rashes? Incriminating photos?*
>
> **Max:** *very tame evening. See you soon*

Tame, huh? I found that hard to believe, but

okay. As for me, the jitters were only getting worse. I'd had a nightmare of me standing at the altar in my dress, facing Max and Patricio in their tuxes. "Who do you choose, Lily?" they repeated again and again. "Tell us who!"

"I choose Max," I'd say and then Patricio would begin yelling, "You are making a mistake, Lily! He will never stand by you! He is not loyal." Max would simply stand there staring at me. Not a word in his own defense.

"Honey," my father peeked into my bedroom, which was now their guest room, "the limo is here."

I stood up, trying to keep my head on straight.

"Oh, baby. You look beautiful in that dress." My father's eyes began to tear. I wore my mother's wedding gown. She and I were the same size—or more accurately stated—she'd been my size when she got married. She'd had to let the hem out a little because I was an inch taller than her, but that had been it.

"Thanks, Dad." I kept my fake as hell smile stuck to my face, and I didn't plan to let it go.

"Oh, honey, stop that. You'll make her cry," my mother warned and then looked at me. "Okay, Lily. See you at the church. Careful not to forget your bouquet and don't wrinkle the dress." She leaned forward and kissed my cheek. "Oh. And don't forget to pause for the photographer when you come inside the church."

My stomach turned to cement. *Ugh. Photographers.* I knew my mother had referred to the one we'd hired for the event, but I knew there'd be more, thanks to her "tight-lipped" friends.

"Got it." I flashed a smile her way and took one last look at myself in the mirror. My brown eyes were a little puffy, but other than that, I looked flawless. I'd done an almost perfect job covering my scars and my long hair was pulled back into an elegant, smooth bun so I wouldn't have to fuss with my long hair today. I'd leave the hair fussing to Max. Tonight. In bed.

During the short ride in the back of the white stretch limo to the church, my father became unusually quiet.

"Everything okay?" I asked.

"Of course."

"Then why do you look like you're going to a funeral?"

He patted my hand. "Someday, your child will grow up, make you crazy with worry, make you proud, and then you'll be watching them get married. It all happens so fast."

"Do you regret any of it?"

"Only having children." He cracked a smile.

"Funny."

"I regret not enjoying it more. We spent so

much time concerning ourselves with you and your brother that we often forgot about our own happiness."

"So you weren't happy?"

"I was. I am. Thanks to your mother, because I always knew no matter what, she would be there by my side. Even through the worst of it."

I tried to imagine the things they'd gone through raising the two of us. A son who would never walk and a daughter who made people stare.

"Well, you did a great job." I petted the top of my bouquet—one white lily surrounded by baby's breath, wrapped up in pink satin ribbon. "I'm talking about me, of course. John is an idiot, but there's nothing to be done about that." I cracked a smile.

My father laughed. "Well, looks like we're here. You ready, honey?"

"Ready." I felt calm and comforted by my little chat with my father. It made me realize this was only the beginning of a long road ahead for Max and me. But together, we just might get through anything.

I scooted forward on the seat, and my dad reached for the door. A few news crews approached, but I'd been expecting them.

"Go ahead. It's okay," I assured my father. He was no fan of these people whatsoever.

The limo driver opened the door, and my father got out. He held out his hand, and I took it, carefully extracting myself so I wouldn't catch the veil or dress on anything.

Once outside, the news crews crowded us, lobbing their questions. Not wanting to see them or ever look back on this day and remember them, I looked at my father and focused on his glowingly proud eyes. Nothing else mattered. Not even the crowd of onlookers who'd gathered across the street.

Almost to the open double doors, I spotted our photographer waiting, crouched a few yards inside, kneeling in the aisle.

I did it. I made it. Easy sailing from here. I glanced down and noticed my empty hands. *Crap.* "I forgot my bouquet. Be right back." I turned and scurried back to the limo parked curbside and grabbed my bouquet from the seat inside.

Halfway back to the church door, another news crew rushed me.

Fuck, no. Not these guys. They were the same assholes who'd shown up at my apartment when Max and Patricio had gotten into a fight. They were one of those TMZ type programs, only they lacked any morality whatsoever—spying on people through windows, reporting any rumor they heard regardless of the damage they caused. These guys were vermin.

"Lily! Lily! Have you seen the photos yet, Lily?" the scumbag yelled. "How do you feel about your fiancé having an affair with Adeline Taylor?"

I gave the man a disgusted look. *What an asshole.* Seriously, what kind of person runs up to a bride and asks about her groom's exes? I kept on walking.

"Are you going through with the wedding? Did you know he spent the night at her hotel last night and didn't leave until ten this morning? Have you seen the photos of the two of them kissing at the Blue Electric last night?"

His words stopped me in my tracks, and my shock only encouraged them. The Blue Electric was the club Max had been at last night for his bachelor party.

No, no, no. What did he just fucking say? I stared at the ass-faced reporter standing in front of me with a sadistic smirk on his lips as his crew filmed my reaction. They hoped I'd cry for the entire world, didn't they?

Maybe I would.

"Tell me, Lily, how does it feel?" He urged the cameraman closer and shoved the microphone an inch from my face. "How does it feel to know your fiancé cheated on you last night, the night before your wedding?"

I tried to blink away my tears, but his words

felt like a red-hot fire poker through my collapsing heart. After everything that had happened, every tear shed, every moment of struggle, and the promises made, I couldn't believe it had all led to this: emotional annihilation.

The bastard cheated on me?

What did you expect, Lily? Princes don't fall for frogs. Not in real life. He wanted to have a beautiful life, a perfect life. He wanted a beautiful wife and beautiful babies. I couldn't give him those things.

I dropped my bouquet, smoothed down the front of my white dress, and lifted my chin. "It feels like shit." I turned away from the church, ignoring the roar of the press, and got into the limo. Somewhere in the back of my mind, I had heard my father calling me, but I couldn't face him or anyone. I felt crushed. Crushed beyond all belief.

"Drive!" I told the chauffeur.

"Is something the matter, Lily?" I looked up at the familiar face in the mirror.

"Callahan? Where did the other driver go?" I barely remembered what that guy looked like because I'd been so distracted with the wedding, but I knew someone else had driven us to the church.

"The other driver will take your family to the restaurant. Mr. Cole wanted me to drive you two after the ceremony for privacy purposes."

Like sex, I assumed. *Wow, what a thoughtful sonofabitch.*

"Miss Snow, what's going on? Why aren't you inside?" Callahan asked.

"I'm not getting married. That's why. Can you take me to my apartment, please?"

"Of course, Miss Snow. But…are you sure?"

"Your boss cheated on me last night with that fucking bitch Adeline Taylor. So yeah, I'm sure."

Callahan gave me a look. "Mr. Cole was with me all night, Miss Snow. I promise. I drove the entire party to their hotel myself, and I…" He made a strange face and wiggled his head a little.

"And what?" I snapped.

"I carried Mr. Cole to his room. He was passed out drunk."

I looked outside at the crowd gathered around the church doors and my father tapping on the limousine window, trying to see inside.

"Lily, I have sworn never to discuss anything pertaining to Mr. Cole's activities, but I swear to you, that to my knowledge, Mr. Cole has not seen Adeline Taylor once since—well, I can't actually remember the last time. It's been that long."

What the hell was going on?

"Do you have a phone? I need to check something." My cell was at home. I hadn't wanted to carry it around all night, and everyone I cared about was supposed to be with me.

Callahan slipped it from his coat pocket and held it over the seat. I crouched down and grabbed it. I took a seat and typed into his browser "Adeline Taylor and Maxwell Cole."

Immediately, dozens of pics and links popped up. Posted an hour ago. Posted forty minutes ago. Posted two minutes ago. *"Scandal before the wedding night." "Maxwell Cole bangs ex night before wedding."*

I tapped on one of the links and a picture came up. It was Adeline Taylor all right. And she was kissing Max.

Wait. I looked closer. The man wore a baseball cap and sunglasses, similar to something Max might wear if going into stealth mode. His stubble even looked the same. It really looked like him.

I toggled to the next photo, a blurry thing showing the same man rushing across a hotel parking lot.

It was Max. But... "This isn't Max. This isn't Max! Max would never wear a shitty pair of jeans like that. This isn't Max! Why the hell is Adeline running around with some Max look-alike?"

Callahan shrugged.

"Ohmygod. Thank you, Callahan. Thank you so much."

"For what? I only told you the truth, ma'am."

I blew out a breath. "Because I almost fucked it up again." I rushed for the door and pushed.

My father helped me up and out and whispered in my ear, "Lily, what's happening?" We were surrounded by press.

I looked up at him. "I forgot."

He gave me a strange look and handed me back my bouquet.

"I forgot that Max loves me." I deserved him. I deserved him and everything wonderful in my life despite my imperfections. I couldn't ever feel like I wasn't good enough again.

"Of course he does, Lily." My father had this look in his eyes that said, *No duh, baby. No fucking duh.*

I took my father's arm, and he walked me inside the church. The doors shut behind us and music filled my ears. At the far end of the room stood Maxwell Cole in his tuxedo, looking so goddamned beautiful that he stole my breath. His hair a fucking sexy mess, his jawline perfectly scruffy, a crisp twinkle in his hazel eyes despite being hungover. And those sensual, full lips...

Scowling?

Uh-oh...

Max gave me a disapproving look, like he used to do when I worked for him. I now knew that when he got nervous, he immediately defaulted to his pissy-faced mode to hide it.

I walked toward him down the aisle, too happy not to smile. By the time I reached him, he, too, was beaming.

At the end of the aisle, my father kissed me and handed me off to Max. I could hardly contain all of the emotions inside my heart.

"Miss Snow, I see you're still having issues with punctuality," Max whispered. Being late, even by two seconds, was something he used to scold me for when he was my boss.

I grinned, knowing that this time it was his way of saying he was worried as hell that I wasn't going to show.

"Sorry, Mr. Cole. Just had a little hiccup. It won't happen again, sir."

epilogue

Our daughter, Iris, was born in February, exactly eight months to the day after our wedding, and aside from marrying Max, it was the happiest day of my life.

Iris, named after the flower that symbolized faith and hope, was nothing shy of a miracle, and I felt it every time I looked at her. Yes, there was a moment when I laid eyes on her looking all newborn red and alien like, that I wondered if she'd end up like me. I still didn't know. But the moment I held her in my arms, I knew I wouldn't care if she turned out to be a beauty queen or average or just plain ugly in the eyes of the world. Okay, let's be honest, with a father like Max, her odds of turning out reasonably good looking were pretty strong. All that said, she was perfect to me. So, so breathtakingly perfect. And I'd love her always, no matter what. Most importantly, I'd teach her to love herself. I'd make her strong and confident and she'd know she deserved "a seat at the table," as Max liked to say.

However, the best part of all wasn't the peace and joy I felt having her in my arms, but watching Max's expression when he held her for the first time. For eight months, we had worked at LLL and we had planned for Iris. We spent as much time alone as we could, knowing that we needed time together as husband and wife before our lives changed again. We ate out. We ate in. We took weekend trips. We jogged in the mornings. We made love. A lot. In eight months, we made Max's house into a home and opened five new LLL locations. It was crazy and exciting, but every day I woke up hearing Max tell me how much he loved me and how lucky he felt. And I knew we were going to change the world for Iris, and she would never feel ugly.

Iris came in the middle of the night, and Max was a mess, all panicked and trying to be in charge, but having absolutely zero control over what happened next.

"Just stay strong, Lily," he kept saying over and over again. "I love you. You can do this."

"Shut up. You stay strong! You first!" I'd screamed with the terrible contractions.

Then she arrived.

It was like the entire world disappeared, and all Maxwell Cole could see was her. Just her. I can't recall ever seeing a man look at something with so much love. And I could swear that little baby, only a few minutes old, looked right back at him with complete and utter adoration as he held her in his arms.

"Uh-oh," I said. "I think we're going to have a big problem."

Max snapped out of his new-daddy daze, but still had a shit-eating grin. "What's that?"

"You're going to spoil her. I can see it in your eyes."

"I'm going to spoil you first, Lily. You were amazing." He returned to beaming at Iris. "Didn't your pretty mommy do a great job?" He kissed her little forehead and spoke in baby talk. "Isn't dat right, my wittle Iris. We're going to spoil Mommy and you're going to be a daddy's girl."

I laughed. "No way. She's going to be independent and strong like her mom. None of the prissy entitled crap."

Max's face went all serious. "I'll make you a deal; the first one I get to spoil, and you can do what you like with the second one."

I cringed. My body felt like it had gone through a meat grinder. Pregnancy was not my friend right now.

"Why don't we focus on this one, and after I'm healed, I'll race you for her."

Max nodded his head. "A very smart man

did say once that if you wanted something, you had to fight for it."

"Exactly. And, of course, I will so win."

"Because you play dirty." He referred to the fact that he'd made me race him for that trip to Milan. I'd won by pulling my shirt off and sprinting for the finish line. It had been nighttime, but Max had still tripped. I won.

Okay, he won. He'd won me.

"All right. That's enough." I held out my arms. "Let me hold her again before my parents get here."

"Nope. She's mine." Max sat down and started blowing little kisses at her. "Muah! Muah. You love your daddy, don't you?"

Seriously. My heart melted. I could look at the two of them all day. "And to think, I almost walked away from this."

I had come very close to letting my fugly voice tell me lies again, but I'd won the battle. That didn't mean I didn't have more growing to do, but things felt different now. I saw my life and myself more clearly. And I had Max and Iris to thank for it.

As for the rest of the world, I'd learned I couldn't let anything they said or did get between me and the things that really mattered.

Those photos of "Max and Adeline," by the way? What a goddamned scandal. Ready for this? It turned out that Patricio had been producing a movie—his big indie debut. Though they changed the names to Lilah and Mick in the film to avoid getting sued, the movie was about me and Max. That total pig-woman Adeline, of all of the people in the goddamned world, would play me. Some Max look-alike played Max, and Patricio would play himself.

Such a horrible rat turd of a man. In the press, he claimed that what started out as just research—aka pursuing me—for the film turned into true love after a few dates. I suspected, however, it might have been more about the publicity. I mean, let's face it, the paparazzi had conveniently shown up a few times when Patricio and I were together. I also wondered if his desire to marry me was more about his ego than anything else. He wouldn't want to film a movie ending that made him look bad, right? And he definitely saw losing "the girl" to Maxwell Cole as a blow to his ego. Whatever his true feelings, I didn't know, and I didn't care. Because I'd made my choice. I chose Max. I chose me. I chose a good life for Iris.

I looked at Max holding his tiny daughter in his arms and my heart swelled. Life really could be so beautiful. If you just let it.

The End. (Yes. For real this time.)

note from author

Hello, My Beauties!

As always, I want to thank you for reading and hope you got something worthwhile out of reading Max and Lily's story (fun, a laugh, some steamy-fuel, or something to think about). I know this story didn't have the huge twists and turns (or fancy unicorns, LOL) like my other books, but I really wanted to honor the underlying meaning of the first book. I wanted this book to be the continuation of Lily's internal story. I mean, yes, plenty of external events happen to her, but really this was about Lily figuring out how to cope with her fugly voice—the one many of us have, hate with a passion, and would like to shove down a deep dark well. (Raise your hand if you've ever told yourself you're too fat or not pretty or not smart enough. Raise your hand if you've been telling yourself that since you were old enough to know what fat, pretty, or smart were.)

But before I get to the deeper stuff, let's get swag out of the way! I have signed fugly bookmarks (they're actually not fucking ugly, they're kinda cute!) for those who want a little keepsake. First-come basis! Just shoot me your shipping address, full name, and be sure to mention if you posted an awesome review so I can include an IT'S A FUGLY LIFE magnet for your collection as a thank you! (I'm lovin' the pics, by the way, some of you are sending of your fridges covered in Mimi swag. Nice!) Send emails to: mimi@mimijean.net.

All right, now that we have that out of the way, here are some insights about the book. (And for those who love the playlist, don't miss it at the end!)

One, while this story is primarily about Lily not allowing her negativity to degrade the quality of her life or keep her from her goals, the story was also about Lily having to make peace with herself and her fugly voice. Because she'd realized that having her face reconstructed didn't do a darn thing for her insides, she needed to find another way to move forward. She needed to face the truth. And for her that meant accepting she didn't really know how to be honest with herself. She made choices that masked or distracted her from the real issues and emotional pain. Opening a boutique wasn't bad, but she knew she could do better. Patricio wasn't right for her, yet she'd convinced herself he was.

Then Max came back and made her question everything. He represents the truth,

Lily's truth. He represents the happiness, love, and prosperity she was keeping from herself. It was difficult, scary, and painful for her to accept the truth (aka Max), but once she did, she knew it was the only way to live her life with any kind of peace or joy.

As for Max's mom, in the first book (and this one), she represents the fugly voice. She hates Lily, she wants to destroy Lily, she wants to sabotage Lily's chances for happiness with Max. Lily's shrink tells her to make peace with her fugly voice because it's there and it's a part of her, but Lily puts up a fight. And when she violently confronts Max's mother (really her fugly voice), she learns that she's the only one who loses. Fugly wins again, landing Lily in hot water, arrested. And Max's mom is happy to have brought her down. But from that, Lily learns the more attention she gives Maxine, the more power she gives her. When Lily finally makes peace with Max's mom, Lily realizes that she can keep Maxine at a distance, know she's there and that there's a hell of a lot of work to be done to fix Maxine, but that she (Max's mom) doesn't have to get in the way of Lily's happiness. So Lily making peace with Maxine (shaking her hand) doesn't mean Lily likes her, but Lily gets that she can't change reality. Maxine is Max's mom. Lily's fugly voice is there. Deal with it and put it in its place, but don't ever empower it.

Finally, Lily has to accept that she makes mistakes. She's never ever gonna be perfect no matter how hard she tries, but doesn't need to beat herself up. At the end of the story, Lily is once again tested. More lies about Max are thrown at her, just like the first book. And once again, she believes them. She listens to her fugly voice and not to her heart. Won't she ever learn? Won't she ever be perfect and get everything right?

Hell no.

Yes, it would've made a more warm and fuzzy story if she simply hadn't believed the press, but then we'd miss seeing something bigger and better happen. Lily knows she's failed to achieve perfection but doesn't tell herself she's an idiot or a failure for her shortcomings. She simply recognizes she's made a mistake by believing her "lovely lies" and moves on with life and with Max, her truth, her true love, and her future.

Okay, all! I hope you enjoyed this mushy, gushy note, and I hope you enjoyed the story. And now...for something completely ridiculous. God of Wine comes next. And yes, he really thinks he'll save the world with his super abs! Haha!

With LOVE,
MIMI

PLAY LIST:

"Can't Pretend" by Tom Odell

"Magnetised" by Tom Odell

"HandClap" by Fitz and the Tantrums

"Way Down We Go" by Kaleo

"All We Have" by Ok Sweetheart

"Mad World" by Gary Jules

"Made Of Stone" by Matt Corby

"Fake It" by Bastille

"Packed Powder" by Blind Pilot

"Welcome To Your Life" by Grouplove

"Good Grief" by Bastille

"Good Girls" by Elle King

"Usted Me Encanta" by Intocable

"Like Lions" by Blind Pilot

acknowledgements

A heartfelt thank you goes out to my readers who continue to cheer me on and share pieces of their lives. Whether it be your unicorn cookie recipes, your own stories about life, or just simply letting me know that I made you laugh when you needed it most, it's an honor being a part of your lives.

To the folks who help make the books better and make them happen...this was #23! I'm still wondering how many I'll get to torture you with, but I'm hoping it will be many, many more. Thank you Kyle, Dali, Ally, Naughty Nana, Latoya, Pauline, and Paul!

Love,
Mimi

coming soon

god of wine

Coming November 2016!
Book #3 of the *Immortal Matchmakers Inc.*
Series (Standalone)

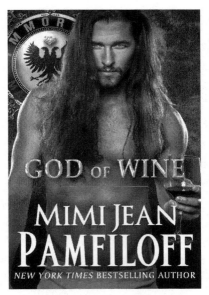

**CAN ROCK-HARD ABS SAVE THE
WORLD? HE SURE THINKS SO!**

Acan, the God of Wine and Intoxication, has been partying for over ten thousand years. And New Year's Eve, when humans around the world succumb to his naturally occurring spike in powers, is his big night. Only this year, things are a bit different.

A plague is sweeping the immortal community, and he's turning downright evil. All those New Year's bashes will turn into bloodbaths if he doesn't stop it. Sadly, the only known cure is finding a mate, and he is a giant, rude, beer-bellied mess. Definitely not husband material.

But can a little gym time and help from the pros at Immortal Matchmakers, Inc., turn him into a divine sex-machine? Absolutely!

So watch out, ladies! The God of Wine is lookin' for love. And he has absolutely no clue what he's doing.

FOR RELEASE DATE NEWS, BUY LINKS, & MORE, GO TO:

www.mimijean.net/godofwine.html

ten club

Book #5, the FINALE of the King Series

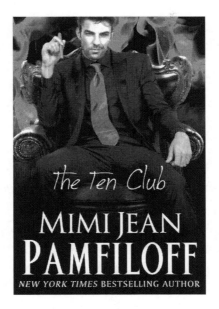

about the author

MIMI JEAN PAMFILOFF is a *USA Today* and *New York Times* bestselling romance author. Although she obtained her MBA and worked for more than fifteen years in the corporate world, she believes that it's never too late to come out of the romance closet and follow your dream. Mimi lives with her Latin lover hubby, two pirates-in-training (their boys), and the rat terrier duo, Snowflake and Mini Me, in Arizona. She hopes to make you laugh when you need it most and continues to pray daily that leather pants will make a big comeback for men.

Sign up for Mimi's mailing list for giveaways
and new release news!

STALK MIMI:

www.mimijean.net
twitter.com/MimiJeanRomance
pinterest.com/mimijeanromance
instagram.com/mimijeanpamfiloff
facebook.com/MimiJeanPamfiloff

Made in the USA
San Bernardino, CA
12 October 2016